WHO IS
STEALING
THE TWELVE DAYS
OF CHRISTMAS?

Books by Martha Freeman

The Trouble with Babies

The Trouble with Cats

The Spy Wore Shades

The Polyester Grandpa

Fourth Grade Weirdo

The Year My Parents Ruined My Life

Stink Bomb Mom

WHO IS STEALING THE TWELVE DAYS OF CHRISTMAS?

MARTHA FREEMAN

Holiday House/New York

In memory of
Jane Browne Petersen
a fine agent
and a finer person

Text copyright © 2003 by Martha Freeman
All Rights Reserved
Printed in the United States of America
www.holidayhouse.com

3 5 7 9 8 6 4

Library of Congress Cataloging-in-Publication Data
Freeman, Martha, 1956–
    Who is stealing the twelve days of Christmas? / by Martha Freeman.—1st ed.
        p. cm.
    Summary: When parts of outdoor Christmas displays go missing from neighborhood
yards, nine-year-old Alex and his friend Yasmeen investigate.
    ISBN 0-8234-1788-3
    [1. Christmas decorations—Fiction. 2. Cats—Fiction. 3. Mystery and detective
stories.] I. Title.

PZ7.F87496Wh 2003
[Fic]—dc21   2002191920

ISBN-13: 978-0-8234-1788-9 (hardcover)
ISBN-10: 0-8234-1788-3

ISBN-13: 978-0-8234-2167-1 (paperback)

The Twelve Days of Christmas

On the first day of Christmas,
My true love gave to me:
A partridge in a pear tree.

On the second day of Christmas,
My true love gave to me:
Two turtle doves,
and a partridge in a pear tree.

On the third day of Christmas . . .

. . . On the twelfth day of Christmas,
My true love gave to me:
Twelve lords a-leaping,
Eleven ladies dancing,
Ten pipers piping,
Nine drummers drumming,
Eight maids a-milking,
Seven swans a-swimming,
Six geese a-laying,
Five golden rings!
Four calling birds,
Three French hens,
Two turtle doves,
and a partridge in a pear tree.

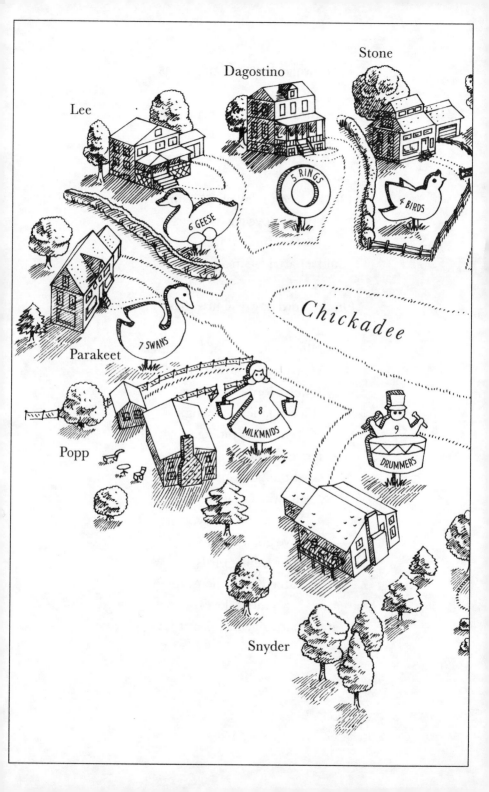

Chapter One

A goose was the first to go.

My cat was the first to notice.

It was Friday morning before winter vacation. I was looking out my window to see if maybe it had snowed overnight. One good thing about Pennsylvania winters—sometimes you get lucky and get a snow day, no school.

But I didn't see a single flake. Only blue sky and the Christmas display in the Lees' yard next door. The Lees are six geese a-laying. On the other side are the Popps, eight maids a-milking.

My family is seven swans a-swimming.

This might not necessarily make sense. So I

will explain. Every December, the people on our street decorate their yards from the carol "The Twelve Days of Christmas." At one end there're the Ryans: partridge in a pear tree. At the other are the Jensens: twelve lords a-leaping.

Really, the partridge is a big rubber ducky painted gold. Glued over the flat ducky beak is a pointy construction-paper beak. The pear tree is a dogwood.

Then there're the lords. They are flat and jig-sawed out of plywood.

The five golden rings are Hula Hoops.

That's reality. But starting that same Friday night, reality wouldn't matter. That night almost everybody in the neighborhood would get to-gether at the Jensens' house. Then Professor Jensen would throw a switch to turn on lights and music. Suddenly, the plywood, the paint, the Hula Hoops—they would all become *Christmas.*

We live in College Springs. It's pretty small. So the Twelve-Day display is a big deal. It's up through New Year's, and practically everybody comes to see it. It's such a tradition that when somebody sells one of the Twelve-Day houses, the decorations go with it. It doesn't even matter if the new people celebrate Christmas.

Since there was no snow that morning, I went ahead and pulled on a T-shirt and sweater. Then I saw the T-shirt stripes were in the back and the tag in the front, so I had to start over. I was twisting the sweater over my head for the second time when Luau jumped onto the windowsill.

Luau is my cat. The windowsill is where I keep my Super Macho Military Mice.

Luau swiped his paw to knock down the Mice. Then he swished his tall and blurted a morning meow.

I thought he meant "Greetings, Alex. I don't believe you've petted me today." But when I petted him, he didn't purr. Instead, he butted his pink nose against the cold window, and he swished his tail some more.

What was he looking at?

Luau has checked out all the Christmas displays. His favorites are ours and the Lees' because they have big, fat birds. Sometimes Luau curls up in a sunny spot by the window and watches them. I know what he is thinking when he watches: "Go on, you tasty birds. *Move.* And the second you do—*eeeeyah!* Thanksgiving!"

But why was Luau meowing and swishing on the windowsill now?

I looked outside again. This time I saw.

"No kidding?" said Dad when I told him. "The Lees are short a goose?"

I nodded. "And it wrecks the whole song, too." I sang: ". . . seven swans a-swimming, *five* geese a-laying, *five* golden rings . . ."

Dad cringed. I guess maybe the grown-ups are tired of that song. "Point taken, Alex," he said. "But who would want a hollow plastic goose? Are you sure it didn't waddle off somewhere? Maybe it's got a nest."

"Or maybe it flew away," I said, "same as that lord."

Last year a blizzard blew the third lord from the left right out of the Jensens' yard. The next day Michael Jensen, who is in seventh grade and the king of the street, snooped around and found him. He had crashed headfirst into some lady's rosebushes.

Dad shook his head. "That goose is too fat to fly. I'll call the Lees when I get the dishwasher emptied. And I'd better do a beak count on our swans, too. Maybe it's the start of a Christmas crime wave."

Dad was making a joke. He and I know all about crime in College Springs. My mom's a police detective. Actually, she's *the* police detective. There has never been enough crime for the police to hire another one.

But the way it turned out, Dad's comment wasn't a joke. It was a prediction.

Chapter Two

Every day Yasmeen comes by at 7:45 to pick me up for school.

When the doorbell rang, I was zipping my coat and tugging my mittens. Doing both at the same time was a mistake. One of the mittens got stuck in the zipper. I had to look down to unstick it, and my hat fell over my eyes. Blind, I tried to open the door for Yasmeen, but what I grabbed wasn't the doorknob, it was an umbrella handle. I yanked; the umbrella came out of the stand; I fell backward onto my tailbone.

Yasmeen pushed the door open and found me on the floor, aiming an umbrella at her.

"Don't shoot!" she said. "I'm on your side!"

"Good morning, Yazzie," my dad called from the kitchen.

"Good morning, Mr. Parakeet," Yasmeen answered. Then she looked down at me. "You're in quite a predicament there, bud."

I scowled, stood up, put umbrella back, removed mitten from zipper, put coat on. I tried to look cool. I tried to look like someone who has been getting dressed by himself for years and years now. Meanwhile, Yasmeen sighed and looked at her watch and sighed again.

"Okay. Ready," I said finally.

"Backpack?" she said.

"Oh, right." I looked around. What had I done with it?

"Closet?" she said.

"Oh, right." I opened the closet door. My backpack was on the floor.

Yasmeen shook her head. "Late as usual," she said. "We'll have to run for it!" And before she even finished her sentence, she had sprinted down the walk.

"Bye, Dad!" I slammed the door and ran after. Catching her was hopeless. Yasmeen is the same age as me, but she's tall, skinny, and fast. Luckily,

I knew she would stop and wait at the corner. It's the same every morning, except I don't necessarily fall on my tailbone every morning.

Yasmeen's last name is Popp—her family is eight maids a-milking, next door. She has a little brother, Jeremiah. Even though she gets stuck baby-sitting him a lot, she says it's good she has him, because only children, like me, are egotistical.

I should get mad when she says this kind of stuff. But usually I am too busy trying to translate. She has this giant vocabulary, which is not her fault. Her father is an English professor at the college. Her mother is a librarian. They are nice but very strict. Like Yasmeen and Jeremiah have to be in bed by 8:30, even on weekends. And they have to make their beds before they go to school.

Yasmeen can be a royal pain. Like she thinks she is saving my life when she comes by to pick me up. She claims if she doesn't, I will get lost and end up dying in the desert of dehydration, which means thirst.

One time I pointed out that there are no deserts in the middle of Pennsylvania. Out beyond Wal-Mart are only soybean fields and cornfields and cows. Beyond that is woods.

Of course, then Yasmeen had to go and remind me about the time she was sick and stayed home. Walking by myself, I didn't pay attention and turned the wrong way at the light. I walked a long way before I started wondering if the school had moved and nobody told me. Finally Officer Krichels spotted me and took me to school in the patrol car, which was just the tiniest amount embarrassing.

I missed the flag salute and the lunch count.

"But I never got lost in any desert," I told Yasmeen.

"Did you have a canteen with you?" Yasmeen said. "A compass? Matches? A flare to signal low-flying rescue planes?"

"No, but—"

"You would have died of dehydration," she said, "desert or not."

Even though she is like this, Yasmeen is my best friend who happens to be a girl. What is good about her is that she is brave and smart and strong. Also, like I said, fast. And even though she teases me and bosses me, she likes me, too.

* * *

Assuming you turn the right way, it is only four blocks to College Springs School. Our street, Chickadee Court, is a dead end. That's the first block. So first we pass the Twelve-Day houses, then, at the corner, the thirteenth house. It's the oldest house on the block and smaller than any of the others. It's where Bub lives.

Maybe in your town it's different. But in College Springs, kids don't have to work hard on the last day before winter vacation. We had our Friday spelling quiz same as usual. We went out to recess and threw snowballs. We had lunch. We got in our math groups. I had finished a multiplication worksheet and was coloring the puzzle when Russell leaned over. Russell loves to blab. He is always getting in trouble.

"Are you coming to my party?" he whispered.

"I told you already I am," I said.

"It's gonna be great," he said. "Mice everywhere! Millions of Mice!"

"Too bad we can't take 'em home," I said.

Russell's birthday party was Sunday afternoon at the toy store downtown, Mega-Menagerie. It was a Mouse party, of course. That's what everybody wants this year.

"I get to have ten kids and peppermint ice cream cake," Russell said.

"You told me already," I said.

"And Mom even let Graham ask somebody. My little brother is so spoiled. I was never that spoiled when I was five."

I looked over at Mrs. Contis to see what she was doing. Mrs. Contis looked up at the same time and smiled.

"Shhh," I whispered at Russell, and I nodded toward Mrs. Contis.

But Russell didn't shhh. "Graham asked Billy Jensen," he said. "Of course the two o' them get along. Billy Jensen is spoiled, too."

"Russell?" I whispered.

"What?"

"Your party will be great. So be quiet! Okay?"

Russell finally got the message. I went back to coloring. The door to the classroom opened and three moms walked in, all carrying trays of food. It was time for the class party! *Yessss!*

My mom was one of the three, the only one

wearing a black police uniform. It has cool stuff like handcuffs hanging from the belt. When they saw her, the other kids in my class nudged each other, and Russell pointed at her gun. This always happens. Sometimes it makes me proud, and sometimes it makes me embarrassed.

"Hi, honey." Mom came over and knelt next to my desk. "I'm really sorry," she said quietly, "but I can't stay for the whole party. Something's happened, and I have to go back to work."

Russell overheard. His eyes got big. "Something *bad*? Like a *murder*?" he asked.

"Not quite that bad," Mom said. But she didn't smile or say no big deal. This was pretty unusual. Most of Mom's cases are missing wallets, cars, and bikes. A lot of times they are lost, not stolen. Mom says it's a good thing people in College Springs are so absentminded, otherwise she wouldn't have a job.

There was no point asking her questions now. Not in front of so many blabbermouths. I figured I would wait and ask her after school. But when I got home, feeling all sloshy with cookies and punch, Mom was still at work. And there was another surprise: Luau was gone.

Chapter Three

My cat Luau was born on the same day as me. Here is what happened:

My mom was drinking tea in the kitchen. I was inside her belly. She heard a horrible howl. It must have startled both of us because she felt the kind of pain that means the baby wants out. My dad had to pack her off to the hospital quick. No time to see what was howling.

But later, when I got done being born, Dad solved the mystery. In a half-open drawer in our mud room was a stray cat licking one sticky kitten.

My mom named the kitten Luau.

And now Luau was missing.

"I let him out this morning," Dad said. "I

thought he was making his rounds. But he didn't come back for supper. It's not like Luau to miss a meal."

Dad put a glass of milk and a plate of Oreos on the kitchen counter for my snack. In my belly, the punch and cookies gurgled.

"Would you mind having a look around for him?" Dad asked me.

I wondered where Luau was, too. But I wasn't worried. Luau is one of those big-shouldered, muscle-y cats. He looks sweet curled up on the sofa, but in his heart he is a tiger. If you don't believe me, I'll bring over the mole guts that prove it.

"I'm supposed to take my Mice over to Ari's," I said. "He got the newest one for Hanukkah. It's a Mongol warrior from the thirteenth century, Genghis Mouse. You should see his weapons, battle-axes, and scimitars; they are *awesome*."

Dad shook his head. "Sometimes I think the Jensens are right," he said.

"What about the Jensens?" I took a sip of milk.

"They won't let Michael and Billy have war toys," Dad said.

"You're kidding," I said. "Not even Mice?"

"Not even."

I couldn't believe it. Michael Jensen didn't own one single Mouse? Did that mean he wasn't so cool after all? I remembered something else, too. Last summer practically everybody got water bazookas—but not Michael and Billy. I never thought about it then, but now I understood. "Gee, that's *mean*," I said.

"I wouldn't call it mean," Dad said. "Different parents have different ideas about raising kids. And the Jensens have a point. There's too much violence in the world."

I don't know about too much violence. All I know is Mice are amazing. I shook my head. "Poor Michael. Poor Billy."

Because you might have been living with no TV on Planet Squelch, I will explain about Super Macho Military Mice. They are little stuffed-animal guys with big pink ears. Each one is dressed in a combat uniform and carries its own tiny weapons. Some of them come with transportation, too—like a horse or a tank. Kids wait in line whenever a new Mouse comes out.

Around Christmas and Hanukkah, grandparents get in fistfights trying to buy the last one.

"You can look for Luau on your way to Ari's," Dad said.

"I'm bad at finding things," I said.

"True," Dad said, "but you might get lucky."

"Besides, Luau's tough. Maybe he caught his own supper."

"Kitty fast food," said Dad.

"Not fast enough," I said, "if he caught it."

Dad laughed. "Good one."

I went upstairs thinking how I liked hearing my dad laugh. He didn't used to so much. Either he was tired or he wasn't around. Till last year he worked 24/7 at this new company that made some kind of software. He and Mom talked all the time about how we were going to be rich, richer than the Jensens—and they have the biggest house on our street and take ski vacations every year.

Rich sounded good to me. But with Dad working so much and Mom's weird detective hours, I spent a lot of time with baby-sitters and at after-school club.

Then things changed. I don't know precisely

what happened, but one afternoon Dad came home and told us he had quit. Now he calls himself a househusband. We don't have people come to clean for us anymore. We don't go out to dinner. We don't talk about getting rich.

Sometimes having Dad around so much can be a pain, like now, when he's telling me to look for my cat. Or when I tell somebody my dad does the laundry, and the somebody looks at me funny. But mostly, I like having him home.

I took my six Mice off the windowsill and put them in my backpack. Some kids have a zillion—the lucky pups. I thought again about Michael and Billy and how they didn't have any. I guessed it was possible to be cool if you didn't own Mice. I mean, if it wasn't your fault. Michael and Billy can't help it if their parents have messed-up ideas.

Anyway, I have only six Mice because I have to buy them with my own money. I was hoping to get more for Christmas. The one I really wanted was Ulysses S. Mouse. The company doesn't make him anymore, so he's practically impossible to find.

Before I ran downstairs, I looked out my

window. Still five geese. By the front door, I stopped to ask Dad.

"I did call over there this morning," he said. "Marjie Lee hadn't even noticed—you know how she is."

"Are they going to replace it by tonight?" I asked.

"She was going to try," Dad said. "But where do you get a big goose on short notice?"

I slung the backpack over my shoulder and walked out the front door. It wasn't that cold this afternoon, and Luau has a couple of favorite sunny spots. One is the porch swing at the Dagostinos'. I looked, but he wasn't there. The second is down the street at the Sikoras'—the birdbath in their backyard. The Sikoras are never home, so I cut back beside their house and looked over the fence.

Nope. Nothing in the birdbath either.

Where can he be? I thought. Maybe I should call Dad when I get to Ari's and report.

I passed the Ryans' house and was rounding the corner at Bub's when something in his window caught my eye. Bub's curtains are almost always closed; you can make out the flicker of the TV set behind them. But this didn't look like a flicker. It looked like an orange tail.

I braked fast. Was that Luau's tail? Why would Luau be at Bub's house? Was it like a kidnapping—I mean, a cat-napping?

Chapter Four

No one is named plain "Bub," but that is the only name I have ever heard for him. He is an old guy. In his driveway is an extra car that never goes anywhere. He doesn't always mow his lawn or shovel his walk. He doesn't put up Christmas lights or play music.

Some of the neighbors call Bub's house an eyesore. According to Billy Jensen, Bub used to be a bank robber, and before that he was a professional wrestler. Billy never said anything about cat-napping, though. And anyway, everybody knows Billy tells stories.

As I stood on the walk in front of Bub's, trying to decide what to do, I figured only three things were for sure. One, Bub is big with a loud, gruff voice. Two, my cat was missing. Three, there was an orange tail swishing in the window.

It all added up to one thing: Alex Parakeet to the rescue!

Too bad Alex Parakeet is a wimp. Unlike my cat, I am not big-shouldered or muscle-y. I am more like small with a round middle. My parents say I am a healthy kid, and this is what healthy kids are supposed to look like. Muscles come later. But what else would parents say? That I look like a party balloon and someday if I'm lucky I'll look like a beach ball? If you know anything about parents, you know this is not how they operate.

I could ask Dad for help, I thought. But I knew what Dad would say. That Bub is a neighbor. That Bub has a gruff voice only because he used to smoke cigarettes.

That I am certainly capable of ringing a doorbell and asking about my own cat's tail.

Aren't I?

I had no choice. I walked up the driveway and up the steps to the porch. I tried to look cool, like someone who has been walking on his own for years and years now.

Then I breathed two times. Then I pressed the doorbell.

Almost instantly the door creaked—I swear—and swung open.

"What do *you* want?"

Bub's voice was as loud and gruff as ever. He was wearing blue jeans and a plaid shirt. My nose came up to his belly, which stuck out over a silver belt buckle.

"My cat," I said.

Bub stepped aside. "Come on in. Soup's been simmering all day. Finally tastes right."

"Uh . . . that's okay." I didn't move. "I mean, thanks, though. Uh . . . *do* you have my cat?"

Bub scratched his cheek. "Let me think," he said. "Big fellow? Orange? Yellow eyes?"

I nodded.

"Seems to me I saw a cat like that somewhere, but—"

A *mrr-oww* interrupted him. Then Luau walked into the front hall, looked at me, and side-rubbed Bub's legs.

"Haven't seen him lately," Bub said.

"Uh . . . but that's him." I pointed.

"Oh, *that* cat? I'd about decided that cat was mine. Today was his turn for the remote. He prefers old movies. I like *Jeopardy!*"

"You mean he comes over a lot?" I asked.

"Last couple days he does. I suspect he's after what I got in the bathtub. Thinks it's cat food, which I guess it would be if he got hold of it. Don't you worry, though. Door's shut."

What was there to worry about? What was in the bathtub? I was working up my courage to ask when Luau meowed again. Then he climbed his front claws up my leg and butted my knee with his nose. His tail was swishing. "He's trying to tell you something," Bub said.

"Yeah," I said. "But what?"

Bub opened the door wider and looked across his driveway to the Ryans' yard next door.

"Well, how do you like that?" Bub said. "Leave it to a cat to notice."

I turned around. And when I saw, my heart bumped. What was going on anyway?

You might not necessarily remember that the

Ryans are partridge in a pear tree. Or more precisely, disguised ducky in a dogwood. But now the Ryans weren't either one. The ducky was as gone as the Lees' goose. The Ryans were just plain tree.

Chapter Five

When I picked up Luau, Bub laughed.

"I'm not sure which o' you is bigger," he said.

Thanks a lot, I thought. But what I said was "Thanks for keeping him."

"No trouble," said Bub. "But remind him how tomorrow *I* get the remote."

I carried Luau over my shoulder, and all the way home he tickled my ear with his whiskers. I thought about Bub. He still scared me. But Luau seemed to like him.

Then there was the missing bird, the *second* missing bird. What was up with that anyway? Would somebody steal fake birds? Why?

At our front step I had to drop Luau to open

the door. I was half afraid he'd run. But he waited politely, then walked inside with his tail flying, his majesty returning from a visit to a neighboring kingdom.

"Back already?" Dad called.

"I brought Luau." In the kitchen I explained how he was at Bub's house, which made Dad laugh.

"Oh—and another bird's missing! The ducky . . . partridge, I mean."

Dad looked up. "You're kidding," he said. "That's not good. The lights go on at six, and it's after four now. I wonder if Beth's home from school yet."

Beth is Mrs. Ryan. She's a first-grade teacher.

By now it was too late to go to Ari's. When I called, he said it didn't matter because Matt Kizer was there, and Matt Kizer had thirty-two Mice.

Ari did not need to mention about all Matt's Mice. Everyone in town knows about all Matt's Mice.

For a second I felt grumpy that I only have six, but then Ari said, "See you at Russell's birthday," and I felt better.

Chapter Six

It's the same every year at the Jensens' holiday party. All the neighbors who put up Twelve-Day decorations go, which means everyone on Chickadee Court except Bub. At six o'clock, Professor Jensen flips the switch that turns on lights and music at all the houses. After that, the kids go down to the rec room, which has a Ping-Pong table, a wide-screen TV, and a huge Christmas tree that is only for Michael and Billy. We eat junk and watch movies and slam Ping-Pong balls. Finally our parents get done with their talk-talk-talk and tell us they're really sorry they kept us up so late, we should have been in bed hours ago.

This year, besides the neighbors, Michael and Billy's grandparents would be there. They were visiting for the holidays, Dad told me. They live over the mountain in Belleburg.

Mom still wasn't home from work, so Dad and I went by ourselves. We were hardly in the door when Yasmeen came over to us, all excited.

"There's trouble with the Twelve-Day decorations!" she said. "Somebody stole them!"

"I know all about it," I said. "But it was only a couple of birds. Luau's the one that discovered it."

Yasmeen was disappointed that I knew more than she did. So she changed the subject. "Are you hungry? I'm ravenous. Let's see if any of the food up here is edible."

We went into the dining room and looked the table over—smelly cheeses, crackers with burnt specks, mini-pie things, mini-riceball things, cookies with lumps, bread with mysterious orange dots, mini-sandwiches full of gooshy stuff.

"Are you thinking what I'm thinking?" Yasmeen asked.

I nodded. "The gooshy stuff looks like toothpaste."

"Toothpaste probably tastes better."

"How can grown-ups eat this?" I asked.

Yasmeen shook her head. "Not even a potato chip."

Besides us, Michael was in the dining room, along with two people I figured were his grandparents. Grandpa was bald. He wore a red sweater. Grandma had bright red hair and wore glasses. Her sweater had green happy faces on it. They each were holding plates piled with shrimp.

Grandma sure seemed to like shrimp, which to me look precisely like naked bugs. Between bites, she did the usual grandma thing—squeezed Michael and cooed at him. Michael rolled his eyes the way any kid would, but I could tell he was trying to be patient.

"Such a lucky boy," she said. "I can't believe all the advantages you have! Big house! Fancy food!" She waved the plate. "We couldn't give your dad all this, you know. Not on what we had in those days. The lock shop never made us a dime."

"I know, Gran," Michael said.

"Leave the boy alone, Gerrie." Michael's grandpa nodded at us. "His friends are here."

Grandma ignored him. "Only thing I wish is that your parents would lighten up on this gun business. Your dad grew up hunting. It's since he met your mom that he's gone all peaceful. There didn't used to be anything *peaceful*—"

"Gerrie?" Grandpa interrupted.

Grandma sighed. "Can't an old woman express her opinion?"

"You're not old, Gran," Michael said.

"Bless you, honey." She gave him another squeeze, then she looked over at Yasmeen and me. "Now, who are these youngsters, Michael? Friends of yours?"

Michael introduced us, and she asked about school the way grown-ups always do. After that it seemed like either Yasmeen or I should ask her something. I couldn't think of anything except maybe how she made her hair that color. But Yasmeen gets more practice talking to grown-ups. Her parents make her go to the Baptist church every Sunday, and she has to stay for doughnuts after the service, too. I went with her once, and all you do is talk to grown-ups. Scary.

"Was that you I saw jogging, Mrs. Jensen?" Yasmeen asked just like she was a grown-up herself.

Michael's grandma grinned. "That was me, all right," she said. "I've never had any luck with money, but I sure as heck keep my body trim. Sometimes it's hard to find the time with this new business of ours, but I do try."

By now the time was after six, and it looked as if the kids would be stuck upstairs with the grown-ups for a while. It was a risky situation— lots of wild, hungry kids mixed with lots of boring grown-ups in a fancy house full of breakable decorations.

But there was something lucky. Sophie Sikora had pulled one of her world-famous temper tantrums, so her parents had kept her home. If Sophie had been here all this time, the Jensens' house would look like a bulldozer had come to visit. She is that kind of kid.

Yasmeen and I went out to the living room and snagged seats on the sofa next to her little brother, Jeremiah. For a while, we sat and watched people talking.

"Hasn't anybody got anything we could use for a partridge?" Mrs. Ryan asked. "Bill tried, but every rubber ducky in town has sold out."

"I've got a rooster ornament on my tree," Mrs. Dagostino said. "Would that do?"

"How big is it?" Mrs. Ryan asked.

Mr. Stone interrupted. "Entirely inappropriate!" he said. "A rooster looks nothing like a partridge."

"Neither does a ducky," Mrs. McNitt said, "and no one has ever complained."

Mr. Stone said he'd been meaning to bring up the matter of the ducky.

Mrs. Ryan said she didn't realize Mr. Stone was a bird authority.

Mrs. Lee wanted to know if it would be all right if the rooster stood in for her missing goose.

Mr. Stone said it certainly would not be all right, and what was this world coming to when people couldn't identify basic birds?

My eyes followed the cup of eggnog in Mr. Stone's hand. The madder he got, the more it sloshed.

"Do you think he'll let somebody have it?" I whispered.

Yasmeen nodded. "I bet Mrs. Lee. She's really exasperating, my mom says."

I shook my head. "I say Mrs. Ryan. Look how her ears are turning pink. She's gonna lose it; he's gonna blast her."

"What if he spills on *us*?" Jeremiah said.

"The last straw was the passenger pigeon—" Mr. Stone said. A few drops of eggnog splashed. Yasmeen and I grinned. This was it. Eggnog cream rinse.

But then my dad had to come over and spoil it. "Now, remind me, Ted," Dad said to Mr. Stone, "where was it you bought those calling birds?"

And of course Mr. Stone explained how he *made* the calling birds. Everyone in the neighborhood knew this like they knew their own house numbers. He told the story every year.

"I can't believe your dad," said Yasmeen.

"What a party pooper," I said.

"It's too bad your mom couldn't come," said Yasmeen.

"Why? She's an even *worse* party pooper."

"That's not what I meant," said Yasmeen. "Where is she anyway?"

"Working. Some big thing, but I don't know what yet."

"Bigger than missing plastic birds?" Yasmeen asked.

I shrugged. "In College Springs?"

Small fingers gripped my knee. I looked down. It was Toby Lee. He was learning to walk. I could see from his frown that it was hard work. First he aimed his body, then he tilted forward, then he moved his legs as fast as they would go. If the legs didn't keep up with the rest of him, he pitched over onto the floor. Then Mrs. Lee would pick him up, or some other neighbor. I have seen Mr. Lee only twice in my life. Mom says he works all the time. Then she always frowns and adds, "That poor woman."

I gave Toby Lee my hand. "Steady, bud," I said. He grinned at me. There was drool dripping off his chin. I turned him and aimed him at Billy Jensen.

"Go!" I said. He tilted, he ran, he was off!

Billy is five. He got a Discman for his birthday. Now the 'phones are permanently attached to his ears. He lives in Discman-land, just him and whatever loud, bad music a five-year-old listens to. So of course he didn't notice Toby till Toby tilted into him with a bump that knocked Billy off balance.

For a second I thought Billy might stay on his feet.

But he didn't.

This was a shame because Billy happened to be standing next to the Christmas tree. The big, fancy, white, for-company Christmas tree. The one with all the fragile ornaments the Jensens don't put on the for-kids tree downstairs.

When Toby hit him, Billy toppled over. Into the tree. Which—*timberrrr!*—toppled over. Needles, balls, and lights shot everywhere. So did the guests. So did the drinks.

"My antique ornaments!" Mrs. Jensen wailed.

"Bring napkins!"

"We need a broom here!"

"Watch out for that glass!"

The grown-ups tripped over each other trying to clean up. Toby Lee was fine. He had fallen onto his diaper-cushioned tailbone. Now he sat in the middle of everything, laughing and clapping his hands.

I bet it was a thrill to be so small and cause so much trouble.

But Jeremiah said, "Someone's going to step on him and squash him like a bug."

I thought Jeremiah might be right. So I pushed through all the grown-ups, scooped up Toby, and set him safe on the sofa next to us.

In a few minutes, the tree was back in place and plugged in. Mrs. Jensen, who has long, pink fingernails and always looks perfect, drank two quick cups of eggnog. Everybody clapped, Toby Lee loudest of all.

Then the doorbell rang. When Professor Jensen answered, Luau strolled in.

"Would you look at that?" said Yasmeen. "You'd think that feline received an invitation in the mail."

"*Ki'y!*" squealed Toby Lee. "*M'ow, ki'y! M'ow!*"

Luau put his nose in the air and sniffed. Then he headed for the dining room.

"Alex?" Dad had just spotted Luau.

"I don't know, Dad. He came in when the front door opened."

What did he want in the dining room, though?

Toothpaste sandwiches? Oh, of course—*shrimp!* I followed, but Luau was sneaky. By the time I got there, he had disappeared. Meanwhile, I could hear Professor Jensen talking to someone at the door.

The voice outside said, "You've got fifty people out there, Jon. They want 'The Twelve Days of Christmas,' and they want it now!"

I forgot about Luau for a second and pushed the drapes so I could see out the window. The first thing I noticed was a white delivery van with a cat's head painted on the side. It said "Tabby Antiques and Junque, Belleburg, Pennsylvania." It had been there a couple of days. It must belong to Michael's grandparents.

Then my eyes adjusted, and I saw the tourists. That's what we call the people who come by to see the decorations. I recognized a few—Mr. Sobel, the gym teacher, Ari's family, the man from the bank. Everybody was bundled up with steam-puff breath. They were clapping their mittens to stay warm. None of them looked precisely joyful.

Mrs. Jensen peered over my shoulder. "Oh, dear," she said, and poured herself more eggnog.

Still at the front door, Professor Jensen tried to explain about the birds' disappearance. The man was not impressed. "Give us one minute," Professor Jensen finally said.

Then he came back to the people in the living room and said, "I guess you caught the gist of that?"

Mr. Stone argued. "Well, I don't care. It's our reputation! We can't light the display when half the flock is missing—"

"Oh, fiddle," said Mrs. Ryan. "Two birds? Give the people what they want."

"Let's put it to a vote," said my dad.

"Point of order!" said Mrs. Popp.

"Can we please get on with this?" said Mrs. Dagostino. "I vote *yes!*"

"Yes!" shouted a lot of people.

"Any noes?" Professor Jensen looked right at Mr. Stone.

"*No!*" said Mr. Stone.

"*No!*" said Jeremiah from the sofa.

Professor Jensen ignored them and turned to Mrs. Popp. "Anita?"

"There ought to have been a motion and a

second," she said, "but given the circumstances—*yes.*"

"That's it, then. The lights go on," said Professor Jensen.

Luau picked this moment to come out from under the dining room table. *"Meow?"* He side-rubbed Michael's grandmother's leg. She had just put a shrimp into her mouth. Its tail hung between her lips.

Gross if you're a kid. *Yummy* if you're a cat.

"Luau!" I whispered.

"Go away!" Michael's grandmother bit off the tail. Then she bumped Luau with her foot.

"Hey!" I said. "Don't kick my cat."

I grabbed for him, but he was speedy. In a flash he had leaped to the bookcase next to the switch for the lights and music.

"Who have we here?" asked Professor Jensen.

"Isn't that your cat, Alex?" asked Professor Popp.

"I'm allergic," sniffed Mrs. Snyder.

"Sorry! Sorry." Dad grabbed Luau off the bookcase and threw him over his shoulder. "Proceed, Jon. Sorry."

Everybody watched, even Luau, as Professor Jensen flipped the switch. Outside, the tourists cheered. The music began, "On the first day of Christmas . . ."

Professor Popp shook his head. "Oh, how I've grown to detest that song."

Chapter Seven

Friday the goose and the partridge.

Saturday a calling bird. Sunday morning a French hen.

Someone was stealing the twelve days of Christmas.

But who? And why?

I had just finished my Sunday breakfast—a bagel with cream cheese. Mom and I were sitting at the kitchen table. Luau was in my lap, purring like he was proud of himself. He was the one who had noticed the missing French hen at the Swansons' that morning. He was starting to think he was some kind of ace detective.

I was happy to leave the bird-watching to

Luau. I had a bigger problem—Russell's Mouse party. It was supposed to start at one, but now it might not even happen.

That's because Mega-Menagerie, where the party was supposed to be, had been burglarized!

Someone had broken in between Thursday night and Friday morning. They stole money out of the cash register. They stole every single Mouse in the store.

Was it possible to have a Mouse party with no Mice?

In case you haven't guessed, it was the Mega-Menagerie robbery that kept Mom busy late Friday. She had worked yesterday, too, looking all over the store for evidence like fingerprints or anything the bad guy might have left.

"Boy, was Mrs. Miggins mad when I made her close her store on the Saturday before Christmas," Mom said.

"Doesn't she want you to find the criminal?"

"Oh, probably," Mom said. "But she might not think it's so important. Insurance pays her either way."

"I've heard of insurance," I said, "but I don't really get it."

Mom explained that most people pay money to an insurance company every month in case there is a disaster like a robbery or a fire. Usually nothing happens, so the company gets to keep the money. That's how it makes a profit. But if something does happen, the company has to pay.

"So insurance will buy Mrs. Miggins new Mice?" I said.

"Right," said Mom.

I thought for a minute. "But it seems like there's a problem. For the insurance company, I mean."

"What's that?" Mom said.

"What if somebody got tired of paying them? What if somebody *pretended* there had been a burglary? So they could get a lot of money . . . or a lot of Mice."

Mom reached over and messed up my hair. "You must be my kid," she said, "because you are so darn smart. What you're describing is called an insurance scam. Somebody fakes a robbery to collect the insurance money. But insurance companies are pretty careful, and so are the police. We try hard to make sure nobody gets away with it."

There was a newspaper on the table between Mom and me. The headline said, "Police Are Baffled."

I looked at my mom. "Are you baffled?"

Mom sipped from her mug of coffee. "So far," she admitted. "But we'll figure it out. Right now what's hanging me up is motive. Why would anybody want those Mice?"

I couldn't believe she had said that. "Are you kidding? Every kid in America wants Mice!"

Mom smiled. "I know you like them, honey. But it wasn't a kid kind of job."

"What do you mean?" I asked.

"When kids break in, they make a mess. Later, they brag to everyone they know. Eventually, you can pretty much count on someone calling to tip us off."

"Are you saying kids are stupid?" I asked.

Mom shook her head. "Not stupid. But not professional thieves either."

"So this was a professional job?" I asked.

"I don't know if it was or not. But it was clean. The thieves got in, grabbed what they wanted, and got out," she said. "In fact, it was pretty remarkable. The door wasn't even damaged."

"Sounds baffling," I said. "What about the birds, though? Any luck with that?"

"Not my problem, thank goodness," Mom said. "Mega-Menagerie's a lot bigger deal. So I handed the birds off to Fred Krichels."

"But he's not a detective!" I said. "*You're* the detective."

"Fred's a fine patrol officer and perfectly capable of looking into a kid prank."

When Mom said *kid*, I laser-stared her the way she laser-stares me when she's mad. But it didn't work. She grinned. "I'm not dissing kids," she said. "Just *some* kids. The ones who have nothing better to do than snatch birds from Christmas displays." She looked into her coffee mug. Empty. "Guess it's time to put my face on and go to work."

"On Sunday?" I said.

She shrugged. "If the bad guys work, then I do, too."

Mom stood up and stretched. Then she started upstairs to put on her "face." That meant lipstick and black eye goop. One time I asked her how come she needed that stuff to be a cop. "Isn't it awful girly?" I said. "I mean, the bad guys won't think you're tough."

Mom had laughed. "I like to think I'm 'girly' *and* tough," she said.

Now Mom called back to me: "You have chores to do, don't forget."

Like I could forget. Since we don't have house cleaners anymore, I do about a zillion chores. Arguing that I'm too young for slavery has not done any good.

I shifted my knees and told Luau his bed was going bye-bye. He dug in his claws and *mrr-ow*ed. This meant "I don't recall giving my cushion permission to move." I scratched him under his chin and behind his ears. "Good kitty," I said. "Smart kitty. Brave kitty. Not to mention brilliant detective kitty."

Luau said *mrrfff,* which meant "How right you are." Then he jumped to the floor.

I got up and cleared the table. Milk dribbled from a cereal bowl. Luau and I cleaned up—me with my sponge, him with his tongue. The phone rang. I grabbed it. "Russell?"

"It's on!" he said. "At Mega-Menagerie."

"Great!" I said. "Hey—but what about Mice?"

"Mrs. Miggins told my mom she's getting an emergency shipment."

When I hung up, I was grinning. This was great and amazing news!

I went back to loading the dishwasher. One thing I have discovered about most chores—you don't need your brain to do them. You can think about whatever you want. So I was thinking how it was surprising that Mrs. Miggins had arranged to get new Mice delivered so fast—especially this close to Christmas.

And I was thinking something else, too. How I really like peppermint ice cream cake.

Chapter Eight

With his tail wagging and his mouth drooling, Leo G. greeted me and Dad at the door to Mega-Menagerie. Leo G. is a St. Bernard dog named after a dead movie star. You have to be careful of him. He doesn't bite, but his slobber is pretty much magnetized to people. Come too close, and instantly you're coated with foamy white dog spit.

Dad backed away, saying, "Good dog, gooooood dog," but he didn't back far enough. Delighted to see us, Leo G. shook his enormous head and the slobber flew—all over Dad's pants.

I laughed till I noticed he had gotten me, too. *Yeccch.*

Dad and I did our best to wipe off as we walked back to the party room. When we got there, I was surprised how normal it looked— Mice on the shelves, Mouse balloons, crepe paper, cake, and the best part, the Mega-Menagerie Mouse battlefield.

"Welcome," Mrs. Miggins said. "I know you've been to Mouse parties before, Alex. You're familiar with the rules, right?"

I nodded. During the party we would be allowed to take Mice down for the war, but in the end we had to put them back—or else our parents could buy them. If somebody damaged one, like he yanked off the tag, Mrs. Miggins made sure his parents bought it.

Dad reached out to shake Mrs. Miggins's hand, but then he must have remembered the slobber, because he pulled his hand back. "Uh . . . sorry," he said. "How are you? The store sure looks great. I can't believe you had a robbery so recently."

"You'd *better* believe we had a burglary," Mrs. Miggins answered. "And it hasn't been easy either. First the *dreadful* shock, then the frantic phone calls trying to find Mice, the clean-up . . .

And at this time of year, too! I've worked my fingers to the bone."

She flashed her fingers, I guess to show their boniness. But what I noticed were three big diamond rings. Selling toys must be a pretty good business.

It's funny about Mrs. Miggins. She owns a toy store but, as far as I can tell, she hates kids. It's like we make her anxious because we might mess up her displays. Dad says in his opinion Mrs. Miggins doesn't like grown-ups so much either. What she does like is St. Bernards—especially Leo G. He stays at the store overnight, like he's some kind of watchdog or something. But I guess he doesn't do much good if the store got robbed anyway.

I joined Matt Kizer and Ari and Russell and a couple of other guys—Sam and Luke—at the cake table. I had brought two of my Mice for the war, along with their trading cards, of course. In case you don't know—how is life on Planet Squelch?—the cards look like baseball cards. On the back is information about the Mouse—his warrior character in history, I mean—including stats like how many battles won and how many battles lost. Ari and I compared General Douglas MacMouse with General Charles George Gordon Mouse. The real General MacArthur was the hero of the Philippines in World War II. General Gordon was the hero of the Battle of Taiping in 1863.

I was sure my Gordon Mouse's tactical smarts would crush Ari's MacMouse in a fair fight, but Ari said no way. Meanwhile, Billy Jensen showed up with his grandma behind him, and Leo G., wagging his tail, behind her. Leo G. is always friendly, but he seemed crazy for Billy's grandma. He had really slimed her good, but she didn't seem to mind. She even gave him a dog biscuit from her pocket.

"How did he know you had that?" Dad asked.

"Know?" Grandma said. "He didn't know, couldn't have."

"Do you have dogs?" my dad asked.

Grandma nodded. "I do. And this guy must sense how much I miss them. My daughter-in-law won't let me bring the dogs when we come. She says they make a mess."

"You were in last week, weren't you?" Mrs. Miggins asked her.

Grandma looked surprised. "Was I?" she said.

"Well, your hair was different, and I don't remember the glasses, but—"

"Not me," said Grandma. "Never been in this store in my life."

Russell's mom clapped her hands to get our attention. Then she said, "Let the war begin!"

Dad looked at me and mouthed, "See you at three."

With the other kids, I dropped to the floor next to the battlefield. Mrs. Miggins made it herself—she is amazing at art—and it is awesome, with grass and tiny trees, mountains and desert, even wild animals. I think the battlefield is the main reason everybody likes having Mouse parties at Mega-Menagerie so much.

I was on Ari and Matt's side with Russell's little brother, Graham. Billy Jensen was on the other team. For once he didn't have his earphones attached. I wondered if his parents realized it was a Mouse party when they RSVP'd. If they didn't like Mice, they wouldn't like a Mouse war. He was probably lucky his grandma had brought him.

We were putting our Mice in position when Sophie Sikora showed up. A couple of guys groaned. I looked at Russell. He nodded at his mom. "She made me," he whispered.

Everybody in town knows about Sophie. She is bad. That's how Mom says it. Dad's opinion is different: A kid might do bad stuff, but that doesn't make the kid bad. We shouldn't put labels on people, Dad says.

I don't know who's right about badness, but Sophie is definitely trouble. She is a year older than me and big. She is not very smart in school, but I hear she always raises her hand because she thinks she knows everything. Usually girls don't care about Mice—Yasmeen doesn't—but Sophie loves them. She has more than anybody except Matt Kizer.

"Come in, Sophie," Russell's mom said. Sophie hung back for about half a second, then charged into the party room. She always moves fast, too fast. On the way to the battlefield, she knocked a chair over and popped a balloon.

"Whose side am I on?" she asked.

"How about the birthday boy's?" said Russell's mom.

"No," Sophie said. "I want to be on Matt's side. With all *our* Mice, we'll *dominate!*"

"Suit yourself," said Russell's mom.

How you play Mouse war is first you set up each Mouse on the battlefield, then you roll dice and draw tactics cards and Mouse cards to see what each number means for each Mouse in each place. Players are allowed to use two Mice at a time. Like in basketball, you can substitute. That's why having a lot of Mice—like Sophie and Matt do—is so good.

Right now, Hanni-Mouse is my favorite. I like his elephant. So I started with him and my own General Gordon Mouse. Later I picked a Sitting Mouse off the shelf. I was careful not to hurt him because I didn't have enough money to buy him.

We were having a great time, and I'm pretty sure my side was winning. We had just overrun the other team's rain forest, and our naval forces were steaming toward their tropical island. Then Sophie had to go and wreck everything.

"My Field Marshal Monty Mouse is tougher than that ol' Alexander," she said to Billy.

You have to remember that Billy doesn't have Mice of his own, and probably never played

Mouse war before. He was still trying to figure out what was going on, plus he's only a kindergartner.

"Huh?" he said.

"I *said*—" Sophie began.

Russell didn't let her finish. "Alexander the Mouse is *too* tough," he said. "Show her, Billy. Here, roll the dice. I'll help."

"Dice are slow," said Sophie, and before our team could stop her, she drove Monty Mouse's tank right into Alexander, knocking him off his horse, off the battlefield, and onto the carpet.

Russell's team couldn't just let Alexander lie there. He had to lead the counterattack! Luke scooped him up, put him back on the horse, and galloped him through our team's forces, slaughtering Mouse allies right and left.

Now everybody was mad.

Matt announced he was going home and started grabbing Mice with both hands.

Graham said Matt stole one of *his* Mice, and sure enough, Matt hid something behind his back.

Sophie climbed over the battlefield, trying to get a look behind Matt's back. On the way she flattened a volcano and slashed a polar ice cap. "Let me see that!" she said. "I think it's mine. *Most* of them are mine!"

"They are not!" said Matt. "You dumb girl!"

Ari tried to get in front of Matt to protect him. But Sophie was quick. She grabbed Matt's shoulder and yanked on his arm to see what he was holding.

"You let *go!*" said Matt. "It's *mine!*" And in the tussle—even though I don't think he meant to—he socked her.

"He hit me! He hit me!" Sophie howled. Blood oozed from her nose.

By now Russell's mom might have been feel-ing just the tiniest amount sorry she had ever invited Sophie. But she didn't show it. In fact, she did the only thing a mom in her predicament could do. She smiled a big bright smile and said, "Time for cake!"

Chapter Nine

On Monday morning I lay in bed extra long and thought about how much I love winter vacation. You never have to put shoes on if you don't want. You hardly have to move from the TV room. Nobody bugs you to go outside and get some exercise. Anyone in his right mind knows it's too cold.

I stared at the ceiling. What to do first?

Movies? Video games? TV?

Popcorn? Chips? M&Ms?

When I got up, I called Yasmeen to see if she wanted to come over and help me celebrate the sofa.

"Well, I am terribly busy," she said.

"Doing what?" I asked.

"Reading the encyclopedia," she said. "I'm up to *I*. Did you know the Incas had gold buildings?"

"Pretty fascinating," I said, "except I don't happen to be Inca. Come over and we can play Lousy Luigi Brothers. It's educational."

"What?"

"I'm serious," I said. "It teaches problem-solving skills. It says so on the box."

"If it's educational, how come you play it all the time and you are still ignorant?" she asked.

"Next to you I'm the smartest kid in our grade," I reminded her.

"Says who?"

"Says everybody! It's a well-known fact," I said.

"Without numbers to back it up, it is mere assertion," Yasmeen said—as only Yasmeen could. "And what's more, it proves my point. You are too ignorant to know the difference."

When Yasmeen is your best friend who happens to be a girl, you learn patience. But now she was pushing it. "Look," I said, "I called to invite you. But you don't have to come."

"Are you serious? I will be right over!" she said. "I am bored beyond belief! Jeremiah is making me crazy. He wants me to play chess with him, but he always wins. And he gets peanut butter on the pieces."

Jeremiah is only four, but he is also some kind of genius. Their whole family is like that. Yasmeen's dad came to the United States from an island I can never remember. He has this cool English accent that would make him sound smart even if he wasn't as smart as he is. Yasmeen's mom grew up really poor. Her ancestors were slaves, which is just so hard to imagine. How could people do that to other people? Mrs. Popp was the first one in the whole history of her family to go to college. She worked really hard to get there, and that's what she expects from Yasmeen and Jeremiah, too. That's why she's so strict.

"Okay, great," I told Yasmeen. "See you in a few."

We hung up. Dad came in with the groceries. I helped him put them away. He had bought Mountain Dew. Yasmeen says it's bilious and won't drink it. More for me.

The doorbell rang. I answered it. There was a burst of frozen air. Then a burst of Yasmeen. "Avian alert!" she said. "Come on! Get your shoes on. Get your coat!"

It was warm in the house. No way was I going out. And what did "avian" mean anyway?

"*Bird*, for goodness' sake!" Yasmeen said. "It means *bird*. From the Latin *avis*. Any kindergartner knows that. Now, come on!"

I planted my feet. "Bird alert? So what are you saying?"

"If you will come outside, you will see," she said.

"It's *cold*!" I said.

"You're a *wimp*," she said.

"I am *normal*," I said.

"What is that supposed to mean?" she said.

"Yazzie?" Dad called from the kitchen. "Is that you?"

"Hi, Mr. Parakeet," Yasmeen answered. "Your son is a wimp."

"Not my son." Dad came into the hallway.

"Thanks, Dad," I said.

"No problem, Alex. So, Yazzie, what's with this wimp business?"

"According to him, it's too cold to go outside," Yasmeen said.

Dad looked at me. "Alex, you are such a wimp. It's beautiful out! Sunny and bright and—"

"—twenty-seven degrees," I said.

"You exaggerate," said Dad. "There's been a warming trend. I'll bet it's up to freezing."

Luau does this thing where he scratches the door with his front paws, only he curls his claws under so they don't catch. The sound is *bump-bump-bump-bump-bump,* like somebody pounding with both fists. Luau was doing this now, wanting to be let out. I could see I was going to lose this argument. All three of them were too much for me.

I tried delaying. "What avian alert?" I asked. "Is another bird missing?"

"Mmm-mmm." Yasmeen pursed her lips and shook her head.

"What, then?" I said.

"Go on out and see." Dad practically shoved me.

I put my coat on. I tied my shoes—slowly. I tried not to look at Yasmeen's smug face. I opened the door; Luau slithered past. Outside on the front porch, shivering and turning blue, I asked again. "Okay, I'm out. Now, what's an avian alert?"

Yasmeen didn't say anything, she just nodded at the Lees' house. I looked over. What the heck? Yasmeen was right. Avian alert!

Chapter Ten

I counted twice and got the same number both times. There were supposed to be six geese a-laying. Since Friday there had been only five.

Now there were six again!

I felt like the newspaper said—baffled. But at the same time I was mad at Yasmeen for dragging me out here. I could have seen the Lees' yard from my bedroom window. And I would have been a whole lot warmer. So I acted like I didn't care. "Maybe it got mixed up," I said. "Maybe it thought it was time to migrate—fly south or wherever, then it turned out not to be, so it came back. Mystery solved."

Yasmeen rolled her eyes. "Alex, you know someone stole that bird," she said, "and someone brought it back. Now, the question is—"

I interrupted: "The question is: How soon can we go back inside and play Lousy Luigi Brothers?"

Yasmeen punched my shoulder. "The question is *who*? Not to mention *why*?"

"I have an idea," I said. "Bribe Jeremiah with a big peanut butter sandwich. Then he will play detective with you. But not me. Mom's the detective in my family. You can tell because she's got the stuff. Police handcuffs. Police walkie-talkie. Police *mittens*."

We were standing in our yard, among the swimming swans. With the lights at night, they look magical. In the morning they look like what they are, white plastic birds on a blue tarp.

We kept arguing. Yasmeen said if I had a shred of curiosity I would want to help her solve the mystery. I said there would be plenty of mysteries to solve in the nice warm summer. Meanwhile, Luau jumped the hedge between our house and the Lees'. Then he started side-rubbing the birds.

I think that before he ate them he wanted to make friends.

Finally, Luau stood up with his paws leaning on a goose's shoulders—if geese have shoulders. The goose was big but lighter than Luau. It fell on its side. I could see the black hollow under its feet. There was something else there, too.

Yasmeen was talking about brain rot—mine, not hers. I ignored her and walked toward the goose. I stepped over the hedge and didn't trip. Yasmeen followed. I knelt by the goose. Inside the hollow was a piece of cardboard dangling by a plastic thread.

"It's just the price tag," Yasmeen said. She tugged and it came away. "Huh, that's strange." She gave it to me. It was a price tag, but not for a goose. It was for Ulysses S. Mouse, Civil War Hero, $9.95.

"You don't have that one, do you?" she asked.

I shook my head. "I sure wish I did. It's from last summer. They sold out right away. Now they're almost impossible to get."

"I wonder what its tag was doing inside a goose," Yasmeen said. "Does Toby Lee have it?"

"Yasmeen," I said, "Toby Lee is a baby. Mice are *not* for babies."

"Sor-*reee*," Yasmeen said. Like my mom, she does not get Mice. "Anyway, what would a Mouse's tag be doing in a goose?"

"I wonder if this was the goose that migrated—that left and came back?" I said.

Yasmeen looked up at the others. "I can't tell," she said. "They all look alike. But if it *is* the same one, then this is our first clue."

"*Your* first clue," I said. "You are the detective, not me."

Yasmeen ignored me. "Come on. We have work to do." Then she turned her back and walked toward the sidewalk, sure that I would follow her. I didn't, though. I stood there fooling with the price tag and being mad. Finally, I stuck the plastic thread in my zipper pull so the price tag hung down off my jacket.

Yasmeen kept walking. I thought about my earlobes. After they froze, would they fall off? Luau looked from me to Yasmeen and finally trotted off to catch up with her.

"Come back here, you traitor," I said.

Now I was standing by myself in the Lees' yard. I felt stupid, like a duck among the geese. What the heck, I thought. Maybe Yasmeen was right. Maybe something else had happened. Something really mysterious. I didn't want to care, but I did. So I gave in and jogged after her. I had almost caught up, when behind me I heard three sounds fast—a skid, a *thud,* and a choked voice saying, "*Oof.*"

I turned around. There on the pavement were Michael Jensen and his bicycle. Of course his bike was the nicest in the neighborhood— fast and red with a plastic crate on the back for carrying junk.

"Are you all right?" Yasmeen was beside him in an instant, of course. You don't let Michael Jensen lie in the street. Even Luau seemed concerned. He circled once, then sat down and watched Michael, tail swishing.

Michael sat up and shook his head. "I'm okay, yeah," he said, standing up. "I don't know what happened. I was riding along . . . then I was on the ground." Michael shook his head again, then he yawned.

"Maybe you need more sleep," Yasmeen said.

Michael nodded. "That's for sure. This paper route is killing me." He pulled his bike back up. Yasmeen and I helped reattach the crate.

"I didn't know you had a paper route," Yasmeen said.

"I'm just a sub," Michael said. "The regular guy is on vacation. I have to get up at four. It's tough." Michael swung his leg over the seat, then he looked at me, then he stared at me. "What's that thing?" he asked. "Hanging from your zipper?"

I felt embarrassed. "It's a tag. You know. A price tag."

"It's from a Super Macho Military Mouse," Yasmeen said.

"Really?" Michael said. "I've never seen one before. My parents . . . you know. Do you mind if I look at it?"

"It was in the goose," Yasmeen explained. "Maybe the one that was stolen from the Lees."

"You're kidding," Michael said. "How weird is that?"

"Alex and I are *detecting*—"

"No, we're *not*," I said.

Michael smiled. "Hey—I thought I was the detective in the neighborhood. Wasn't it me that found the lord last year? Would it be okay . . . I mean, would you mind giving me that, Alex? I'm investigating the birds, too. It might be a clue."

I did kind of mind. This was probably the closest I'd ever come to having my own Ulysses S. Mouse. But I couldn't think of a good reason to say no. Especially to Michael Jensen. So I nodded okay.

Michael put the tag in his pocket. "Thanks," he said. Then he rode off toward his house, and Yasmeen and I continued walking up the street. Luau followed.

"Michael is smart and all," Yasmeen said, "but I don't see why he should be the only detective around. I don't see why we can't solve this case ourselves. Faster than him, too."

"Oh, sure, Yasmeen," I said.

"Seriously. Maybe you shouldn't have given him our clue."

"Why not? Were we going to dust it for fingerprints?"

"Maybe your mom could've," Yasmeen said.

"Mom doesn't even think the birds are

important," I said. "She's totally working on Mega-Menagerie."

By now we were at Mr. Stone's house. Without having to say anything, we stopped, looked over the fence at the display, and counted. One-two-three calling birds. Still one missing.

The Swansons' house was next door. We stopped there, too, and counted: One-two-three French hens.

Wait a minute.

Three!?

Yasmeen looked at me. "Another bird returns," she said.

I shook my head. "Totally weird," I said.

"Totally mysterious," she said. "Come on."

This time we both ran and both skidded to a stop in front of the Ryans' house. Yasmeen looked up at the dogwood tree. Then she looked over at me. She was grinning. *"Voilà!"* she said, which is pronounced "wah-lah" because it's French and French people can't spell. Anyway, it means *There it is!*

Yasmeen pointed at the tree. I expected to see the replacement partridge. It was black because Mr. Ryan didn't have any gold spray paint. It looked like a crow, which must have been confusing to the real crows that hang out on our block.

Anyway, *"voilà!"* there was the plastic crow. But *"voilà!"* again—the old gold ducky was back, perched on the branch below.

Yasmeen shook her head. "You know what Alice in Wonderland said?" she asked me.

"I don't need to know," I said, "because you are about to tell me."

Yasmeen grinned. "You're right about that, bud. What Alice said was 'Curiouser and curiouser.'"

Chapter Eleven

While Yasmeen and I puzzled over the latest ducky migration, Luau trotted to Bub's and did the *bump* thing with his paws. Pretty soon Bub opened the door, and Luau disappeared inside. Then Bub waved at Yasmeen and me.

"He wants us to go over," I said.

Yasmeen's mom is one of the neighbors who calls Bub's house an eyesore. Yasmeen shook her head. "I can't," she said.

"Come on," I said. "You can't get in trouble for standing on his porch."

Yasmeen didn't look sure, but she still followed me across the driveway and up the steps.

"What're you kids doing out in the cold?" Bub asked.

Now that I had talked to him once, I felt braver. "Yasmeen and I are detecting," I said. "I don't like it much. But she thinks it's great."

"The missing birds?" he said. "I saw this morning that the partridge was back."

I could imagine the wheels turning in Yasmeen's brain. She wanted to leave. She was afraid of getting in trouble. But the urge to detect was stronger. "What time did you see it?" she asked.

Bub scratched his cheek. "Let's see. I got up to start the soup at about six forty-five. But I wouldn't have looked out the window right away. I got the newspaper, turned on the TV, opened the curtains. That'd be when I saw the bird. The sky was getting light—say seven or seven-fifteen."

Yasmeen looked at me. "So whoever it was returned the bird really early—or else in the middle of the night."

"In the dark," I agreed, "after Professor Jensen turned off the Twelve-Day lights at eleven."

"Wouldn't you kids like to come inside?" Bub asked. "Soup'll be ready soon. Chicken noodle."

The soup smelled good. But I knew Yasmeen wasn't allowed. "We have to go home," I said. "But thank you."

"Did you notice anything else suspicious?" Yasmeen asked.

"Well, now that you mention it, yes," Bub said.

My heart bumped. This could be important. "What was it?"

Bub looked right and left like he didn't want anybody to overhear. "A couple o' real peculiar characters," he whispered, "peering into my neighbor's yard."

"Really?" Yasmeen asked. "When?"

"Just now," Bub said. "Two kids. They looked *suspiciously* like Yasmeen Popp and Alex Para-keet." Bub laughed and laughed.

Yasmeen looked disgusted, which was how I felt.

"We already know *we* didn't do it," I said.

Bub was still chuckling. "Sorry," he said. "I can never resist a joke—gets me into trouble sometimes. Besides, how do *I* know you didn't do it? Maybe all this detecting is part of your cover-up. Who would suspect the detective was the criminal?"

I didn't know how to answer that, but I didn't have to. A car pulled into the driveway. A young woman opened the door and climbed out of the driver's seat. She waved at Bub, then went around to the trunk and retrieved a picnic cooler.

Bub moved to come down the stairs. "Let me help you with that," he called.

But she waved him away and hauled it up the stairs herself. She was small, and it was big.

Bub introduced us. "My niece, Jo," he said. "She's a student at the college."

"Did you come for soup?" she asked us. "All my money goes for tuition. I'd starve without Bub. Is Al here yet?"

Bub shook his head. "He's slow today. All the holiday deliveries, I guess. I don't see how anybody can stand Christmas. I hate it myself."

Bub *hated* Christmas? That was weird. I love it—well, mostly what I love are the presents. I wondered if that was what was in the cooler— heaps of presents for Bub. But that couldn't be. Didn't Jo just say her money went to tuition?

"Uncle Bub." Jo said it like a warning. "We've been through this already. This year your Christmas is going to be different." Now she bounced up and down and hugged herself. "Cold out here. Let's go inside. Is the soup ready?"

"Uh . . . we have to go," Yasmeen said.

"What about Luau?" I asked.

Bub leaned back so he could see into his front room. "Sleeping," he said. "But don't you worry. I'll wake him for the movie classic. It's *The Maltese Falcon*. Right up his alley."

Yasmeen and I were at the foot of Bub's driveway when Al pulled up in his red-and-yellow truck. He owns Al's Delivery Service, and that means he brings a lot of Christmas presents. Most of the time on our street he's going to the Sikoras' house. He's Mrs. Sikora's brother—which makes him Sophie and Byron's uncle. This is convenient because they get so many toys.

I always love it when Al pulls up in front of our house.

"Got anything for me?" I called.

"I got something for the Lees," he said. "From Decoy Decor. New goose maybe?"

Yasmeen and I cracked up. A seventh goose. Just what the neighborhood needed!

Chapter Twelve

We were halfway down the block when Yasmeen looked at her watch. "Oh, my gosh, my mom will kill me," she said.

"What? Why? Because Bub has cooties?"

"Not that. I'm late to baby-sit Jeremiah." She ran a few steps, then turned and ran backward. "Promise me one thing."

"Sure, what?"

"Promise you won't do any detecting without me. You won't even *think* about the case. Is it a promise?"

This was an easy one. "No problem, Yasmeen. I'm not going to think about anything this afternoon. I'm going to play Lousy Luigi till my brain turns to mush."

Dad had left me a note—"Back at 2." Since it was past lunchtime, I poured barbecue chips into a bowl and got a can of Mountain Dew from the fridge. Then I settled in on the sofa for the perfect vacation afternoon—sloth and snacks.

But it turned out Lousy Luigi wasn't that much fun. My hero guy kept getting vaporized by evil Pond Scum guys. It was my own fault. I couldn't concentrate. Even though I had promised Yasmeen, I kept thinking about the missing birds.

My mom is a good police detective, but the more I thought, the more she had to be wrong. She said stealing birds was a kid prank. But she also said that kids are messy and they always brag.

That didn't describe whoever was doing this. Whoever it was had a plan. They took only birds, nothing else. They took only one bird at a time. They took a different bird from a different yard every time. They didn't mess anything else up.

Oh—and they returned the birds. At least they had returned three of them.

Did that mean they would return the calling bird, too?

Late in the afternoon Mom called and talked to Dad. She had to work late downtown. There was new information in the Mega-Menagerie Mice burglary. She didn't have time to tell about it then. She was on her way to the library.

"The library?" Dad said.

"Don't wait up!" she said.

Dad and I ate dinner. Fish sticks with macaroni and cheese, a Dad specialty.

"You know what, Alex?" Dad said. "Mom sounded happy when she called. I almost think she wishes there were more crime. I guess some people are born detectives."

"Not me," I said. "I hate detecting."

Dad looked surprised. "How do you know you hate it?"

I explained how Yasmeen and I had spent the morning.

"I think detecting sounds fun," Dad said.

"But be careful. What if there's a desperate bad guy out there? What if you run into him some dark night?"

"Dad?" I said. "What desperate bad guy do you know that steals fake birds?"

Dad shrugged. "I don't believe I know anyone who steals fake birds."

Luau jumped into Mom's chair and poked his nose over the edge of the table. He sniffed; he purred. *Mmm, fish sticks—how I love them!*

"*Shoo!*" said Dad. "Get down, you!" He tipped the chair to make Luau jump to the floor. Luau is always so cool; he acted like being tipped onto the floor was his own idea. He arched and stretched and wiped his face a couple of times. Then he came over and sat by me.

I knew what he was hoping. Very sneaky so Dad wouldn't notice, I shoved half a fish stick off my plate and then off the table. Luau crouched, pounced, and bit it in the neck—not that fish sticks have necks.

"Uh . . . Luau?" Dad had seen the whole thing. "It was already dead. You buy them that way."

"Great, Dad," I said, "there goes his self-esteem."

Dad laughed. "I don't think anything would damage *his* self-esteem."

We cleared the table. Then Dad asked me to help him clean up. "It's valuable father-son bonding time," he said.

"You've got to cut it out with the parenting books," I said.

"And let you get ahead of me?" said Dad.

I flicked my towel at him. He held up a butter knife to defend himself. We danced around the kitchen in a fake fight. Then Dad grabbed the towel from me and waved it like a truce flag. "I surrender!" he cried. "But you still have to help me clean up."

"I need a new dish towel," I said. "This one's used."

The one Dad handed me had a Christmas tree on it. Just seeing that tree made me smile. Three days till Christmas! Then I thought of Bub, and I asked my dad, "Did you know Bub hates Christmas?"

"I know he's no fan of the Twelve-Day display," Dad said.

"Why not?"

"Can't say for sure. Thinks it's silly maybe?

And some people have bad memories of Christmas. From what I hear, Bub grew up pretty poor. It might have been a tough time of year for his family."

"Billy Jensen says Bub was in jail once," I said.

Dad shook his head. "I don't think so. As far as I know, he's just a big, loud old guy who likes to make soup. No crime in that."

I remembered something else about Bub. "What does he keep in the bathtub?" I asked.

"The bathtub?" Dad laughed. "No idea. Why?"

"Whatever it is, Luau wants it," I said. "That's why he spends so much time over there."

"Why not ask Luau?" Dad said.

"I tried," I said, "but he's not talking."

That night I went to sleep early. I guess I hadn't adjusted to the vacation time zone. Next thing I knew, Luau was walking back and forth across my belly. I rolled over, but he meowed. I pulled the covers over my head. He started batting things off my bedside table: the alarm clock, my rock collection, two books.

"Would you cut it out?" I said. "Go to sleep!"

But instead, he jumped from the bed to the windowsill.

I thought of how he'd been acting lately—Luau, the ace detective. Was he trying to tell me something now?

I pushed back the covers, sat up, and looked out my window. It was after eleven, so the display lights were off, but I could just make out the geese in the Lees' yard. One . . . two . . . three . . . four . . . five . . . six . . . No problem. But as I stared, I saw something move. Was it a shadow? But hadn't it looked kind of, well . . . solid?

Luau touched his nose to the glass. Had he seen something, too? Something more than a shadow? I got out of bed, put my face against the window, and cupped my hands around my eyes to see better. There it was—by the hedge between the Lees' yard and ours. It wasn't so shadowy this time. It had a definite kind of person quality. A small-person quality. A kid?

Whatever it was seemed to be crouching by the hedge. And . . . was it carrying something? It looked like it. And whatever it was, it was moving away. Soon I wouldn't be able to see it from my window.

Luau meowed again.

"Okay, okay, I'll go." I slid my slippers on and grabbed my bathrobe off the hook; I ran down the stairs; I opened the front door. A few dandruffy snowflakes floated in on the freezing air. I barely noticed. I was focused on the black shape running out of our yard, past the swimming swans, toward the sidewalk. It was carrying something. I couldn't *see* what, but somehow I knew what. To make sure, I counted.

Yep. Our seven swans were only six.

Chapter Thirteen

It was dark, no moon, only spooky shadows and snow sparkling in the air. Chickadee Court was empty except for the Tabby van down by the Jensens'. The shape had run in that direction, so I did, too. I slipped on an ice puddle but kept my balance. I tried not to think about anything—my freezing toes, my thudding heart, my aching chest. I tried to think only about the shape—where it had gone, how I could catch up. It was almost like playing Lousy Luigi, except I didn't have a joystick.

Also, there was nobody to give me extra lives.

I followed the shape to Mr. Stone's, then I lost it in the trees between the Swansons' and the

Sikoras'. For a moment I stood still and breathed. I was tired. Maybe the shape was, too? Maybe it was resting? But then I saw something moving by the corner of the house. I wished I had thought to grab a flashlight. It was maddening out here in the dark and the shadows. Every falling snowflake was suspicious.

Over there—hadn't something moved again?

I ran to get a closer look, but not too close. What if it turned and came after *me*? It was small, but I was smaller. What if it punched me out? And left me lying in the snow? To freeze?

My coming near must have spooked it. I heard leaves rustle and shake, a branch crack, footsteps padding away. Finally, the shape broke through the shrubs ahead of me and leaped over the hedge. I tried to follow but without a joystick my leaping skills are limited. I had to run all the way around the hedge, and by the time I did that, the shape was only a dark blur bobbing in the distance. What the heck? It was backtracking—on its way toward my house again.

All I could do was follow. A minute later, panting, I stopped in front of the Popps' house. The shape had disappeared here, maybe into the front yard. I stood and looked over the gate. I felt funny about opening the latch and going in, though. Wouldn't that be trespassing?

But sure enough. I saw something black bounce up behind a milkmaid, then duck. It was wearing something black to cover its face. A ski mask?

So much for not trespassing. I unlatched the gate and pushed it open. I was glad the gate didn't squeak. I ran on tiptoe past the first row of milkmaids. Nobody there.

I peered over a milkmaid in the second row. Nothing. Then—there it was! Or was it? I looked from maid to maid. They were all alike. Which one did I want? Not this one, not that. . . . I swear I looked behind every milkmaid and behind the cow, too.

Nothing.

I started running back toward the gate; but halfway across the yard I kicked a bucket—*clank . . . clatter-clatter.* . . . I tripped and fell to my knees, sure I had awakened every family on Chickadee Court.

How would I explain what I was doing in the Popps' front yard? Chasing what? A *shape*?

Because my cat saw it out the window? Somehow I didn't think Yasmeen's parents would understand. *I'd* be the one in trouble, and all for this dumb detecting.

Still on the ground, I rubbed my knees and looked out at the sidewalk. The shape had disappeared altogether. At least there was no sound from the house, no lights blinking on.

I put my hands down on the ground to help me back to my feet. And what I felt there wasn't frozen grass like it should have been. It was something else. Actually, two something elses, one under each hand.

What the . . . ?

I clenched my fingers around whatever they were. I brought them close to my eyes to see them in the dark. But even before I saw, I knew.

Two Super Macho Military Mice.

My brain had been zipping along, but now it froze.

If there were two, were there more? This was like winning the lottery!

Greed took over. I stuffed the Mice in my bathrobe pockets and crawled around the frozen front yard, feeling for more. Pretty soon I had found three—five total. They all must have spilled out of the milkmaid's bucket. But what were they doing there in the first place?

I brushed the area with my hands one more time—no Mice, but there was something else. . . . It felt like a rolled-up piece of paper. Probably just litter, but I stuffed it in my bathrobe, too.

I stood up and brushed the damp dead grass off. Two seconds ago I felt miserable. Now I was so happy! Wasn't this my just reward for running around in the cold? For risking my life and my toes?

I *deserved* these Mice.

I heard the rumble of a car. Then headlights swept across the Popps' yard. I dropped back to my knees, heart pounding again. Maybe I should hide behind a milkmaid. After all, I was trespassing. Plus now I had these Mice in my pocket. I didn't know where they had come from. But I knew they weren't mine—not really.

I also knew I wanted to keep them.

The headlights shone into the yard next door, our yard. I couldn't get through to the Snyders' on the other side. So, on hands and knees, I crept back to the gate, unlatched it, and crawled out onto the sidewalk. In case you ever wondered, frozen ground is hard on the knees. Damp and aching, kneeling on the sidewalk, I tried to decide what to do, where to hide, but suddenly it wasn't up to me anymore. The car moved, the headlights swung toward me . . . and then they stopped.

No point trying to hide now. I was trapped in the headlights—just like a rabbit.

The car door slammed. The headlights stayed on. I didn't want to think about how ridiculous I must look—kneeling on the sidewalk, snow falling around me, wearing my bathrobe and slippers. I tried to see what was coming, but the headlights blinded me.

Another black shape, this one grown-up size, emerged out of the glare.

"Alex?" said a familiar voice.

"Mom?"

"Alex, what are you doing?" Now she was close enough to block the glare, and I could see her face.

"Uh . . . that would be a little hard to explain."

"Alex . . . you're out here in the middle of the night and it's snowing and you don't have a coat on!"

"I know that, Mom."

"Or boots!"

"I know that, too, Mom. Uh . . . could we . . . ?"

She helped me up and pulled me close in a hug, trying to wrap her black police coat around me. It was only then, all scrunched up next to her, that I totally felt how cold I was.

"Your teeth are chattering!" she said.

"Yeah, Mom, I know—could we—?"

"I want some answers, young man. What are you doing out here on the sidewalk without a coat?"

"Uh . . . I didn't have time to grab a coat."

"What were you in such a hurry for?"

"M-m-om." It's hard to talk with chattering teeth. "C-c-could we go in—?"

"Alex, for goodness' sake! This is no time for discussion!" she said. "We need to get you inside."

Mom half shoved, half carried me to the car, then opened the door. An orange flash scooted in ahead of me. "L-L-Luau?" I said. "W-what are you doing here?"

Luau blurted a small meow, and I swear it meant "Chasing bad guys, of course. What else would I be doing?" Then he settled in the front seat next to Mom.

She looked at him and shook her head. "The gang's all here."

Instead of answering, Luau washed his face.

Five minutes later I was in my bed with Luau purring on my feet. Mom came in. She was still wearing her uniform. My bathrobe, Mice in the pocket, was hanging on the hook on the back of my door. Even though it was my own mom, there was something scary about a police officer walking in right then. I felt a pang of guilt.

"Alex," she said, very serious. "I had a horrible thought. You're not the one, the kid, I mean . . . you haven't been . . . ?"

I knew right away what she meant. "No, Mom," I said. "I didn't steal the birds. Honest. I was out there trying to find out who did." Now that I was warm, I told her about Luau meowing, about the shape, about our missing swan. I did not tell her about the Mice.

When I was done, I yawned. So did she.

"It's contagious," I said.

"It's two in the morning," she said.

"But what did you find out?" I asked. "Why did you have to go to the li—" The "brary" dissolved into another yawn.

"Go to sleep now," she said. "We will talk tomorrow." She turned out the light by the door.

"Mom?" I mumbled. "Do you believe me?"

"Yes, honey, I do," she said, and there was a smile in her voice. "Your imagination's not that good."

Chapter Fourteen

Yasmeen rang the doorbell at 7:45 that morning, Tuesday. She had to ring twice and practically sit on it the second time. Where was Dad? Where was Mom? I was so sleepy I just about tumbled to the door.

"What are you doing here?" I asked. "It's vacation. Did you forget?"

Yasmeen barged in, closed the door, and took off her mittens. "Would I forget?" she asked. "I'm here now because I have to baby-sit later. And did you see the latest avian alert? One of your very own swans is missing!"

I nodded. I wanted to tell her the whole story, but it was too big an effort. I yawned instead.

"Have you had breakfast?" Yasmeen was disgustingly wide awake, which is what happens when your parents are strict about bedtime. "I had oatmeal," she said, "but I could use a snack. Is there anything good?"

We went into the kitchen; she opened the cereal cupboard. I sat down at the table, rested my head on my hands, and closed my eyes. I guess I dozed because the next thing I heard was slurping. Yasmeen had poured herself a bowl of cereal. She always slurps the milk at our house because she's not allowed to do it at home.

"This stuff isn't bad." She nodded at the box of Marshmallow Pirate Treasure. "But it could use more of the pink marshmallows. Are you awake yet?"

I shook my head to clear out the sleep. It more or less worked. "Yasmeen, there is so much you don't know," I said. "I almost froze to death! I got practically no sleep!"

"Uh-huh," she said. "What were you doing? Chasing bird thieves in the middle of the night?"

"Yes!" I said. "That is precisely what I was doing!"

Yasmeen couldn't decide whether to believe

me. "Okay," she said slowly. "I'm listening. Start at the beginning." She poured another bowl of cereal and milk. But she didn't eat it. She was too amazed.

I told her everything, well, almost everything. I kind of left out the part about finding the Mice. Yasmeen wouldn't understand why I deserved them. And I didn't want my best friend thinking I was some kind of thief.

When my story was done, Yasmeen stared.

"Say something," I said. "Tell me I'm an idiot not to have caught the shape—or at least gotten a good look."

Yasmeen shook her head. "I don't think you're an idiot," she said. "I think you were kind of . . . brave."

I thought she was kidding. No one had ever called me brave before. I guess for the good reason that I never was. "Brave?"

"Chasing down a bad guy?" Yasmeen said. "In the dark and the cold? The middle of the night? You could've gotten hit on the head . . . or frostbitten . . . or lost!"

"Yasmeen, I was on our own street."

"Doesn't matter," Yasmeen said. "*You* could've gotten lost."

"And besides, I didn't catch him."

"It's intentions that count, bud. But you do have to promise me something."

"What?" I asked.

"Next time you'll take me with you."

I grinned. Yasmeen was telling me I was good for once. It felt great. In the back of my mind was one bugging-me thought, though: Maybe she wouldn't think I was so great if she knew I had all those Mice in my bathrobe.

"There's something else, too," I said. "It's probably not important. But I found a piece of paper on the ground in your yard—with the milk-maids. I haven't looked at it yet. Let me go get it."

The paper was still wadded up in my pocket with the Mice. I pulled it out and brought it downstairs.

"It looks like printer paper," Yasmeen said.

"It looks like trash," I said.

"Not in *our* yard," Yasmeen said. "Go ahead and open it up."

"You," I said. "It's your turn."

Yasmeen used her palms to flatten the sheet of paper. The ink had run in places, and all the creases made it hard to read.

Hard but not impossible.

For a moment Yasmeen and I were speechless. What the heck did *this* mean?

On the table was a map of Chickadee Court. It looked like it had been drawn by a not especially great artist—maybe a kid. The map showed the thirteen houses, each labeled with its family's name and the name of its Twelve-Day decorations. Bub's house wasn't labeled at all.

At the top of the map was a title: "Happy Hunting!" There was a smiley face underneath.

But here's the most interesting thing, the thing that made Yasmeen and me stare: Some of the houses were marked with black X's, and with numbers: 1, 2, 3, 4, 5.

"It looks like a treasure hunt," Yasmeen finally said.

I nodded. "From a birthday party or something."

"Let's be logical," said Yasmeen. "Somebody was telling somebody where to look for something."

"That's logical." I nodded. "It's not necessarily brilliant, but it's logical." I looked longer and noticed something else. "The X's—they're only at the houses with birds, see? The Lees', the Ryans' . . ."

"And wait a sec—check this out!" said Yasmeen. "The numbers—the Lees' house is one, the Ryans' is two, Mr. Stone is three, the Swansons' is four, and you're five. . . . That's the same order that the birds disappeared in."

"There's no six," I said, "so I guess the crime wave is over."

Yasmeen thought for a minute. "But not the restitution wave," she said.

"The what?"

"Restitution is when somebody pays you back," she said. "The goose, the ducky, the French hen—they all came back. Mr. Stone's calling bird is still missing, and your swan, of course. Aren't they due to come back, too? If the pattern stays the same?"

I thought back to last night. The shadow had grabbed the swan and run off. I was pretty sure about that. But had it been carrying the swan the whole time? Or did it drop it somewhere? I had gotten the best look in the Popps' yard when I was closest, when I thought I saw the ski mask. I didn't think it had been carrying anything then. So had it dropped the swan before it got to the Popps'?

And if so, was the swan still out there?

Chapter Fifteen

It was still freezing cold. A few hours ago I had nearly lost my toes chasing a black shape. I had gotten about a half night's sleep.

Imagine how thrilled I was to be going outside to hunt for my own plastic swan.

"And what if we find it?" I asked Yasmeen. "What will it tell us?"

"I don't know." She pulled her hat down over her ears. "Ready?"

Our plan was to retrace my route from last night. In our front yard I counted the swans again. Yep. Still six. We started down the sidewalk toward Mr. Stone's house. Only a dusting of snow had fallen overnight. There were footprints here and there; some must have been mine; some must have been the shape's. There was a faint bike-tire track on the street. That must have been Michael's from when he delivered newspapers earlier. But there was no obvious trail for Yasmeen and me to follow. The wind had messed everything up.

As we walked, I thought really intelligent thoughts. Like how I was glad to be wearing snow boots instead of slippers. And how it was time for the Dagostinos to touch up the paint on the five golden Hula Hoops.

But Yasmeen's brain never quits. She was thinking about the case.

"If it's a treasure map, someone must have been looking for treasure," she said.

"What?" I said. "Oh, right." I tried to concentrate. The best I could do was "Fake birds aren't a very good treasure."

"Exactly!" she said. "So here's what I think. It was some treasure hidden *inside* the birds. They were all hollow, right?"

I thought for a minute. "Hollow, yeah. But the rubber ducky is dinky. Plus it doesn't have a big hole in its bottom the way the other ones do. You'd have to cut the bottom out or something."

Yasmeen shrugged. "Maybe the treasure is dinky, too?"

"You mean a small treasure inside each of the birds . . ." I said, "and whoever it was took them, looked inside, and returned them?"

"Yes!" said Yasmeen. "That explains it! Why the birds come back!"

This was so brilliant that I stopped walking. For a second it seemed like Yasmeen had solved the whole thing. Then I realized there were just a few tiny details we didn't know yet. "Did they find what they were looking for?"

"I don't know."

"And *what* were they looking for?"

"I don't know that either," Yasmeen said. "And here's another question: Who are 'they' anyway? And for that matter, who's the other 'they'?"

"What other 'they'?" I was confused.

"There's the 'they' who was stealing birds. And the 'they' who made the map. Two different 'theys.'"

So much for solving the whole thing. I was back to baffled. I started walking again. Yasmeen was grinning. "Isn't this fun?" she said.

"No!" I said. "I *hate* thinking this hard!"

"Oh, don't be such a loser. I bet we find that swan. Then we'll have another clue. And meanwhile we should think about what other clues we have. What about the price tag for the stupid Mouse?"

I thought of something. And as soon as I thought of it, I thought what an idiot I was for not thinking it sooner. Then I thought of how I couldn't tell Yasmeen. Then I thought of how much I hated not being able to tell Yasmeen.

I did so much thinking, it must have showed on my face. Yasmeen looked over and said, "What's the matter?"

I shook my head. "Nothing." I sealed my lips.

"Well, it is certainly *something*." she said. "Because you look like the old woman who swallowed a fly."

I shook my head again. I was afraid to open my mouth. If I did, I would tell her everything. I wasn't used to keeping secrets. I didn't think I was going to be very good at it either.

We stopped at Mr. Stone's gate. Three of the four homemade calling birds were in their tree, where they belonged. They really did look good, even in daylight. They were handmade out of papier mâché. Now his kids were grown-up, and his wife was dead. He lived in this big house by himself.

"Where did the shape go from here?" Yasmeen asked.

I showed her the trees by the side of the house, where it disappeared. I pointed at the hedge it had hurdled.

"Wow!" said Yasmeen. "Did you jump over the hedge, too?"

"Not precisely," I said.

"I still think you're brave," she said. "And since you're brave, you can be the one who rings Mr. Stone's doorbell and asks for permission to go swan-hunting."

"What?!"

"Alex, be reasonable. We can't swan-hunt without asking," she said. "Especially at Mr. Stone's. He'll yell at us!"

"I used up all my brave last night," I said. "Your turn."

We argued. Pretty much Yasmeen always wins when we argue. But this time no one had a chance to win. In the middle, Mr. Stone opened his front door.

"What's all the racket? Can't an old man enjoy a winter morning in peace?"

Someone had to say something. Since Yasmeen didn't, I was elected: "Sorry! Uh . . . we were just wondering—" I started to explain about the swan, but Mr. Stone cut me short.

"It's uncivilized to converse at this distance. If you have something to say, come on up here. You, too, Miss Popp."

On the front step, I picked up Mr. Stone's newspaper and handed it to him. Then I started over again explaining. Now Mr. Stone said it was too cold to keep the door open, we'd better come inside. We were both scared, but we went. It was dark in Mr. Stone's front hallway. It smelled sweet, though, like maybe he was cooking something. I explained fast. At the end, I said, "Would you mind if we looked around your yard for the swan?"

Mr. Stone said he had no objection. Then he surprised us.

"In my experience," he said, "there are two kinds of people, those who like marshmallows in their hot chocolate, and those who like whipped cream. I come down firmly on the side of marshmallows. What about you?"

For a minute I thought poor Mr. Stone might be the tiniest amount cuckoo. Then I realized that the sweet smell was hot chocolate on the stove, and the question made more sense.

"Marshmallows," I said.

"Marshmallows," said Yasmeen.

"Then you are in luck," said Mr. Stone. "Because I just bought a fresh bag. Come on in the kitchen."

While he fixed us hot chocolate, Mr. Stone told us his grandchildren preferred whipped cream. He blamed his daughter Susan for this. Obviously she had done something wrong in raising them. Still, the grandchildren were coming for Christmas, and he supposed he would have to purchase some whipped cream. The kind in the can was what they preferred. Mr. Stone shook his head sadly.

Yasmeen took a sip of her hot chocolate. Then her doughnuts-after-church training kicked in. "Is Susan the same daughter that made the calling birds?"

"We all made the calling birds," Mr. Stone said. "But Susan's was a little different from the others. She insisted it had to have pink eyes! There was no reasoning with her. So pink eyes it has."

"I never noticed," I said.

"No, you wouldn't from the street," said Mr. Stone, "only close-up. I hope the thief is amused."

"You mean that's the one that's missing?" Yasmeen asked.

Mr. Stone nodded. "I'm glad you two are investigating at least. Perhaps you'll find a clue. With all due respect to your mother, Alex, the police don't seem terribly interested. That one officer came and took a report. I haven't heard a thing since."

By now we had finished our hot chocolate. "Look around all you want," Mr. Stone told us. "But do keep your voices down for an old man. Won't you?"

Outside, Yasmeen took charge. "It will go faster if we split up. You try the trees over by the Swansons'. I'll try by the corner of the house, where you saw the shape last."

Looking wasn't so easy. The trees were close together. Their branches drooped and tangled. I grabbed one and shook, which got my hands all sappy, and besides, the needles stabbed me. I crawled on the ground to see underneath in the dark. I picked up a stick and poked around. My hands turned black from dirt. My knees were cold, damp, and bruised.

I found a lot of pinecones and somebody's old flat beach ball from summer. I found a Barbie doll's foot, which was creepy. What happened to the rest of her? I shook an abandoned bird's nest out of a tree. I bothered a gray squirrel. He came out on a branch to scold me. He looked a little like Mr. Stone.

But I didn't find any swan. And besides, all this searching proved what I kept saying: Except for the hot chocolate, detecting was no fun.

When I couldn't stand it anymore, I went to find Yasmeen. She wasn't by the corner of the house, so I walked around. In the backyard were an ancient rusty swing-set and overgrown rosebushes. There was a hedge on the other side of the house, next to the Dagostinos'. I jogged alongside it and back to the front yard.

Where had Yasmeen gone anyway? I didn't want to yell because I didn't want to bug Mr. Stone. But this was ridiculous. Had she gone inside for something? Had she gone home without me? Why would she do that?

Talk about being a lousy detective. Now I couldn't even find my own partner.

Finally, I decided to go home myself. Maybe she was there, and if she wasn't, I could try calling her house.

At my house I dashed up the walk past the swimming swans. The newspaper was still on the front step, which told me my parents weren't up yet. I picked it up. I stopped. Something was wrong.

I mean, something was right.

Wasn't it?

I turned around and stared at the blue tarp. One-two-three-four-five-six . . . *seven*! Our missing swan had flown home.

Chapter Sixteen

"What do you mean, where was I?" Yasmeen said. "Where were *you*?"

She was on the phone, calling from her house. I was in the kitchen, eating breakfast at last. I had told her about the swan being back. Now we were accusing each other of ditching.

Meanwhile, I finally heard shoe thumps upstairs in my parents' room. I looked at the kitchen clock: 10:30. It must be nice to sleep in, I thought. Of course, I wouldn't know.

"You are the mixed-up person," I told Yasmeen, "because I was looking for *you*."

"Well, you weren't doing a very good job of looking," she said. "I knew Mom would kill me if

I was late to baby-sit Jeremiah again. I tried to find you, but I couldn't. So I left."

"I looked for you in Mr. Stone's backyard," I said.

"I looked for you there, too," she said.

"And I was crawling around on my knees," I said.

"I was crawling, too!" she said. "Look, I think I see what happened. You must've been looking for me at the same time I was looking for you. We were circling Mr. Stone's house, both going in the same direction but never in sight of each other."

I agreed Yasmeen was probably right. But while I was agreeing, something was bugging me. I couldn't get a handle on what it was, though, because, as usual, she was busy running my life.

She had to make a peanut butter sandwich for Jeremiah's mid-morning snack. After that, her dad would be home, grading finals, and she could come over to my house. We would take a look at that swan to see if there were any clues like price tags or treasure maps. We would tell my mom what we had found out so far. Maybe she could help us? Maybe the police knew something?

When Yasmeen hung up, I sat and stared at the treasure map. Something was still bugging me.

Then I nailed it: our conversation with Bub.

Bub had been teasing us. He said maybe *we* were the thieves. Maybe our detecting was just a cover-up.

Well, I knew *I* was innocent.

But what about Yasmeen?

Till today I never would have thought of Yasmeen. But hadn't she ditched me just now? And ditching wasn't like her either. And wasn't it Yasmeen who suggested we split up when we searched for the swan? And Yasmeen who said I should go over by the trees?

Yasmeen was fast and about the right size. What if she were the shape? *If* she was, then she knew the swan was in the bushes by Mr. Stone's house because she had put it there. And what if this morning she had grabbed it and run back to my house? What if that was why she wanted to go over to Mr. Stone's in the first place?

My brain was very excited. It was going a million miles per hour.

It was also going crazy. Yasmeen was my best

friend. She was wacko sometimes, but she wasn't a thief.

Or was she?

At 11:30 Yasmeen's dad got home and liberated her. She rang the doorbell. We both went outside to look at the returned swan. I reached to pick it up.

"Wait!" Yasmeen said. "What about finger-prints?"

"But I'm wearing mittens. And the thief would've, too. It's freezing out here."

Yasmeen nodded. "You're right," she said. "Go ahead."

I lifted the swan. From its weight I could feel there was nothing in it. I wondered if it had been full of Mice last night. I turned it over. No price tags inside. Nothing inside.

"That's disappointing," Yasmeen said. She looked around on the ground. "What about foot-prints?"

She isn't sounding like a thief, I thought. The thief wouldn't want me to look for footprints, would she?

Brain, I said, *cut it out!* Yasmeen is not the bad guy, she is my friend. I am not going to suspect her anymore.

"The ground's too hard for footprints," Yasmeen was saying. "And there's not enough snow."

"Same as the sidewalk earlier," I said.

Yasmeen sighed. "Two dead ends in a row," she said. "And I thought we were going to solve this case, too."

"Come on," I said. "Let's talk to Mom. Maybe she can help us."

Mom was in the kitchen, making coffee. She had her uniform on; her wet hair was dripping on it.

"You two were up early," Mom said. "I thought you'd sleep till tomorrow, Alex."

"And we've already been out detecting!" Yasmeen announced.

"Detecting?" Mom said. "Well, that's good news. Maybe I can retire to Hawaii at last." She yawned. "So tell me, what is it you've detected?"

Mom sat down at the table with her coffee. She leaned her head on her hand. Yasmeen filled her in—the avian alerts, the map, what the map seemed to mean, the swan's disappearance and return.

As Yasmeen talked, I got worried. What if she said something about the price tag? If Mom saw a connection between the Mega-Menagerie case and the missing birds, she'd take our case over herself. That wouldn't be fair. We'd done so much work. I was surprised I felt that way, but I did.

Mom pulled the map toward her and studied it. "This is *really* peculiar," she said. "But it reinforces my opinion. It's kids. Who else would come up with a dopey idea like a treasure map?"

"Kids are not dopey," I said.

"Sorry, honey," she said. "I didn't mean that the way it sounded."

I thought she meant it precisely how it sounded. But it wasn't worth it to argue. I had to distract Yasmeen from telling about the price tag. So I said, "What did you find out about your case yesterday, Mom? Were you at the library so late?"

"The library first. Then I went and talked to some folks at the local antiques society. They'll talk your ear off, those people. Anyway, you won't believe it." Mom looked up at us. "Remember I couldn't figure out a motive for the Mega-Menagerie burglary? Who would want all those Mice? But yesterday I heard from a detective over the mountain. There was a similar burglary there, and he shared something he turned up. Sometimes those Mice are valuable!"

I rolled my eyes. *"Moooom . . ."*

"What, *'Moooom'*?" she asked.

"You could have talked to any kid on the planet and found that out! Super Macho Military Mice are *collectible*. Especially the retired ones—the ones they don't make anymore."

"What does 'collectible' mean?" Yasmeen added.

It was nice to explain something to Yasmeen for once. "It means they get more valuable as they get older. Matt Kizer even keeps his in plastic bags. He says he wants to corner the market, or something like that. It means he'll own so many retired Mice, he'll be able to sell them for as much as he wants."

"I had no idea Matt was such a businessman," Mom said.

"Maybe you should talk to him," I said.

"Why?" Mom asked.

"Maybe he had something to do with the robbery," I said.

"That sweet little Matt Kizer?" Mom shook her head. "I told you already. It wasn't kids."

"Hey—wait—Ulysses S. Mouse is retired, right?" Yasmeen asked. "So there's a big coincidence, too. Yesterday Alex and I found—"

I kicked her. What else could I do? Not hard, though.

"*Ow!* Why did you—" Yasmeen started to ask, but my laser look interrupted her.

"So what did you need the library for, Mom?" I tried to act cool, like someone who has been kicking his best friend for years.

Mom looked at Yasmeen. Then she looked at me. "Why did you kick Yasmeen, Alex? What am I missing?"

"He didn't kick me, Mrs. Parakeet. I . . . uh, banged my shin on the chair. Sometimes I am such a klutz."

Mom's face was suspicious, but she went ahead and answered. "I needed the reference librarian to help me find current prices on antiques."

"Antiques?" I said. "But Mice aren't old."

"There's old and there's *old*," said Mom. "A lot of antiques stores deal in used stuff—fast-food toys, lunch boxes, baseball cards, even Mice."

"So did you find out what Mice are worth?" I asked.

"A lot!" Mom shook her head. "Really, I think people are crazy. Some of those retired Mice have sold for a thousand dollars. But they have to be in perfect condition—absolutely clean, the price tag still attached."

I cringed when she said "price tag." Would Yasmeen try to bring it up again? But no—one kick had been enough.

"So what do you do next, Mom?" I asked.

"I'm going to make a run over the mountain," she said, "take a look at the store that was burglarized, talk some more to that detective, see what he's got. In the meantime, you kids need to call Officer Krichels. He's going to be interested in that map—and in your little adventure last night, too, Alex. You may have seen the bird thief, or the silhouette of the bird thief. He'll want a description."

"But, Mom," I whined, "the birds are *our* case."

Mom smiled. "I'm not saying you have to quit detecting. There's not much danger investigating a prank. But you two have to share your information with the police. In fact, it's breaking the law if you *don't*. It's called withholding evidence, and you could get in trouble."

Yasmeen did not want to get in trouble. "We'll call him," she said.

"Good." Mom gulped the last of her coffee and stood up. "Oh—and by the way, Alex?"

"Yes, Mom?"

"Do *your* Mice still have the price tags?"

"You said collecting Mice was crazy," I said.

"It is. But if crazy people want to pay crazy sums . . ."

"Yeah, Mom," I said. "My Mice have price tags."

Mom smiled. "Great. And you might want to think about keeping them in plastic bags, too."

Chapter Seventeen

Mom left. Dad appeared. He looked puffy-eyed and pale. He hadn't shaved.

"Are you okay?" I asked.

"Your mom has got to cut it out with these late nights," he said. "I can't sleep till she gets home. And worse yet, she's drunk all the coffee. I'm going downtown to buy a cup. Can you survive on your own for a while?"

"My dad's home," said Yasmeen.

"We're fine," I said.

"We're detecting," said Yasmeen.

Dad padded down the hall toward the garage. Luau jumped onto Yasmeen's lap and blurted a meow.

"He's trying to tell you something," I said.

"He probably wants a treat," she said. "That's all felines ever think about, food."

"That is so unfair," I said. "They think about other things. They think about naps."

"Yeah," said Yasmeen, "and when they nap, they dream about food. Like yesterday? When Luau knocked over the goose? It might have looked like he was detecting. But really he wanted to see if the goose was edible."

Luau meowed again. I thought it meant "Speaking of big, tasty birds, let's go hunt some!"

But Yasmeen heard something else. "Oh, my gosh!" she said.

"What?" I said.

"Your feline reminded me about the goose! We've been trying to figure out what the treasure is, right? What's inside the birds? But all along we *knew* what was in the goose!"

"Price tag," I said.

Yasmeen nodded. "*Mouse* price tag," she said. "And if the map is a treasure map, and if the treasure was inside the birds . . . it must be Mice that are the treasure! Now that I know they're valuable, it all makes sense!"

Yasmeen was proud of herself. I would have been proud of her, too, except, of course, I already had figured this out. I couldn't let on, though, so what I said, all innocent, was "Oh?"

Now Yasmeen looked crushed. "Aren't you going to tell me what good detecting that was?"

"Sorry," I said. "It was very good detecting."

"You don't sound like you mean it," she said.

My conscience was eating me up. I knew more than Yasmeen, and I wasn't telling her. I was withholding evidence. But if I told her everything, she would never let me keep my Mice.

"You might be right," I said slowly. "Maybe Mice *are* the treasure. But we still don't know the who. *Who* wanted Ulysses S. Mouse?"

"Well, for example," said Yasmeen, "there's you."

I felt my heart bump and my face turn pink. *"I didn't do it!"*

Yasmeen looked surprised. "Of course you didn't."

What an idiot. Now my face felt red. I squinched my eyes shut. "Yasmeen," I said, "I have to tell you something. No, wait—show you something."

I went up to my room and came back carrying my bathrobe. Yasmeen gave me a funny look. I didn't say anything. But one by one, I pulled the precious Mice out of the pocket: Napoleon BonaMouse, Robert E. Mouse, Attila the Mouse, GeroniMouse, General George Washington Mouse.

Yasmeen looked at them, then looked at me. "Where did you get those?"

I told her.

"And you were going to keep them?"

I nodded.

Yasmeen crossed her arms over her chest. "And I was so proud of you for being brave!" She looked like a mom. "This is *really* disappointing."

"I shouldn't have told you."

"Oh, yes, you should have!" she said. "One Mouse price tag might be a coincidence—but all these Mice? This proves the connection. Whoever stole the Mega-Menagerie Mice had so many, they gave some away. They made a treasure map, for goodness' sake. And gave away Mice as treasure."

My feelings were all messed up, but my brain was in overdrive. It didn't want to worry about what a rotten human being I was. It wanted to solve the puzzle.

Yasmeen must have felt the same way. Normally, she would have told me five times that I'm a loser. But today she didn't bother. She went right back to work.

"The question is," she said, "what kind of person makes a treasure map?"

"A kid?" I suggested. "That's what my mom says."

"It sounds wrong to me," Yasmeen said. "I don't know, but . . . I think we need another clue. And"—she stood up—"I know just where to look."

"The Ryans'," I said.

Yasmeen nodded. "Great minds think alike."

I looked down at the Mice. "What do I do with these?"

"You can't keep them," Yasmeen said.

"I know."

Yasmeen smiled. "Put them back in your bathrobe. Later you have to give them to your mom, though. I guess you didn't think to dust them for fingerprints?"

"Give me a break, Yasmeen! It was the middle

of the night and snowing! I was not thinking about fingerprints!"

Yasmeen shook her head. "I don't know, bud. At this rate, you'll never make it as a criminal *or* a detective."

Chapter Eighteen

We were all coated up to face the frozen world, when I thought of something. "Hey—we still have to call Officer Krichels."

Yasmeen let go of the doorknob. "Shoot. Do we have to do it now?"

I shrugged. "We said we would."

"We didn't say *when* we would."

"Now who's withholding evidence?" I asked.

"Oh, go ahead," she said. "But it's not fair. We did all the work. We have it half figured out. Now some *grown-up* is going to come along and take credit."

I was afraid of the same thing. But we still had

to call. We had evidence in a police case—two cases if we were right about Mega-Menagerie.

I dialed the phone. Angie Price, the dispatcher, answered: "College Springs P.D., please hold." There was a click, then violins.

"What's happening?" Yasmeen asked.

"Telephone music," I said.

Yasmeen nodded. Angie Price came back. "May I help you?"

"Hi, it's me—Alex Parakeet."

"Alex! How are you? Where've you been? Are you still the smartest kid around?"

"Not exactly," I said.

"Your mom's out of town today, Alex. I could get her on the cell, though."

"Uh, yeah, Miss Price, I know." I thought of telling her to go ahead and get Mom. I should tell her about the Mice. But I wasn't ready to face that. "I was calling for Officer Krichels."

"Really? Well, okey dokey, then. Wait one." Another click.

"What's happening?" Yasmeen asked again.

"Trumpets," I said.

Yasmeen nodded. Miss Price came back. "College Springs P.D.," she said, "may I help you?"

"Miss Price, it's me, Alex."

"Alex who?" she said.

"Alex Parakeet!"

"Well, that's odd. There's an Alex Parakeet on the other line, too."

"Miss Price—that was me on the other line."

"Two lines at once? How do you do that?"

"No, Miss Price," I said. "I'm only on this line. You were looking for Officer Krichels. Remember?"

"Righty-o," said Miss Price. "Wait one."

More telephone music. This time she came back and said, "Your mom's out of town today, Alex."

"I know, Miss Price. I wanted Officer Krichels."

"Really? Well, that's no good either. He's in conference."

"Okay, then, could I leave a message?"

"Well, aren't we getting grown-up, Alex!"

She said it like being grown-up was great. I wasn't necessarily sure. But I thanked her anyway. "Just say to call Alex Parakeet," I said.

"Okay, Alex," said Miss Price. "I'll let her know."

"Not her!" I said. "Him!"

"Who?" said Miss Price.

"Officer Krichels," I said.

"Not your mom?"

"Right, Miss Price. Officer Krichels is not my mom."

Miss Price giggled. "Well, I *know* that, Alex."

I wasn't real sure after I hung up that the message would get through. Yasmeen thought maybe that was a good thing. "We *tried* to share our evidence with the police," she said. "It's not our fault the police don't care."

She was right. This was good. We were still on our own.

A few minutes later, Yasmeen and I headed up Chickadee Court for the second time that morning. Winter break sure wasn't going the way I'd planned. Way too much being in the cold. Way too much exercise. Way too much thinking.

This time we stopped at the Ryans' gate. There in the dogwood was the gold-painted ducky, the original one. The Ryans had taken the black one down, the one that looked like a crow.

In case you are not quite as brilliant as Yasmeen and I, I'll tell you what we were doing there. Yasmeen and I had both realized the same thing. All the other birds that disappeared were big and open at the bottom, like the Lees' goose. The ducky was different. It was hollow, but closed up. If someone wanted to hide something inside the ducky, he would have to cut the bottom out of it.

We were at the Ryans' to check the ducky's bottom.

I was about to tell Yasmeen it was her turn to ring the doorbell, when something warm rubbed my leg. Luau!

"What is with this cat?" Yasmeen asked.

"He thinks he's some kind of ace detective," I said. "I told you he was the one who noticed the missing birds. And he woke me up last night, too."

"Plus he reminded me about the price tag," Yasmeen said.

"Oh, so you speak Cat now?" I asked.

"*Mee-ow*," said Yasmeen, and I had to admit she sounded pretty realistic.

We went to the door together. Since Mrs.

Ryan is a teacher, I figured she would be home for vacation. She answered the door with a roll of wrapping paper under her arm, a shopping bag in one hand, scissors in the other. A piece of Scotch tape was stuck to her hair.

"We're detecting," said Yasmeen. "We want to figure out who's been stealing the Twelve-Day birds."

"Great, great—fine," said Mrs. Ryan. "Just tell me what you need. What I need's about three more weeks to get ready for Christmas."

"But Christmas is Thursday," I said.

"My point exactly," she said.

We explained we wanted to look at the ducky. We were going to explain why, but she put her hand up. "Have at it. Only don't fall out of the tree. I don't have time for fractures."

Mrs. Ryan closed the door with her hip. Yasmeen and I walked over to the tree to plan our strategy. We decided Yasmeen should hoist me up. I'm a klutz, but I'm smaller and she's stronger. Up I went, with a lot of grunting and stretching. I felt big and marshmallowy in my jacket and mittens. Plus it was confusing to work around the spiderweb of lights.

"Put your knee on that lower branch," Yasmeen said.

I tried, but my knee didn't bend in that direction. So I scrambled my boots against the trunk, trying to push my way up. "I can't," I gasped.

Fur brushed my leg; a tail tickled my nose; claws pushed into my head.

"Hey—*ow*—what? *Luau?!*"

Now he was sitting above me on the branch with the ducky. He meowed, and it meant "Next time, Alex, hire a professional." Swipe went the paw; down dropped the ducky. It bounced off my face before it fell to the ground. It was as cold and heavy as a ducky-sized ice cube.

Yasmeen was so eager to see that she let go of me. It was good I hadn't climbed very high. *"Owow-ow!"* I landed hard on my tailbone.

My best friend didn't even notice. She bent down to get the ducky. She flipped it over. *"Yes!"*

"Let me see!"

Yasmeen held it up. "We were right!" I said. The bottom of the ducky was not rubber the way it should have been. It was glued-on cardboard. I took the ducky from Yasmeen and studied the cardboard. It was plain brown, no marks at all. That seemed unfair. Shouldn't there be a secret code or something?

"Someone cut the rubber out," said Yasmeen. "Then they put a Mouse in and glued cardboard on."

I nodded. "After that, the treasure hunter stole the ducky, took the Mouse out, and glued the cardboard back," I said.

Yasmeen high-fived me. "We are *brilliant!*" she said.

"Except we already knew all that," I said.

"We didn't know. We suspected," said Yasmeen. "Now we know. And we know something else, too."

"What?"

"Whoever stole it was a good tree climber."

"Or else they had a cat," I said.

"Let's ask Mrs. Ryan if she's seen anything unusual," Yasmeen said. "And I hope she's got more construction paper. Look." The fall from the dogwood tree had flattened the fake partridge's beak.

The Ryans' house was messy inside—wrapping paper and gift boxes everywhere. Now Mrs.

Ryan's hands were covered with flour. There was a green streak on her nose. The tape was still in her hair.

We showed her the ducky's bottom.

"Hmm," she said, "looks like he's had a duckectomy."

"He needs a new beak, too," Yasmeen said.

"Later for that," she said. "Anything else you need?"

I asked if she had seen anything suspicious. At the same time Yasmeen asked, "What's that smell?"

There was a funny smell all right. Something cooking? Something burning! Mrs. Ryan slapped her hand to her forehead, leaving a flour handprint. "My famous Christmas cookies!"

We ran into the kitchen. Mrs. Ryan pulled the cookie sheet from the oven. We all stared. They weren't as black as I'd expected.

"No matter," said Mrs. Ryan. "This batch is for Bill's relatives. Hardly a taste bud among them. Now, something suspicious? Not that I can think of. Did you want to take a look at the cardboard, though?"

"We did," I said. "No marks."

"What about the other side?" Mrs. Ryan asked.

Yasmeen and I looked at each other. Forget about brilliant. We were a couple of idiots. "Is it okay?" Yasmeen asked.

"Sure." Mrs. Ryan handed the ducky over. "Poor guy needs a plastic surgeon anyway. One more indignity won't matter. Use a butter knife. Top drawer. I'll just get on with my frosting."

With the knife, I wedged the cardboard off the ducky. It took a few seconds before it popped free. I flipped it over. Mrs. Ryan had been right. This side wasn't blank. It was shiny yellow with a pattern made out of red letters—ADS, ADS, ADS. It was familiar, but for a second I couldn't place it.

Mrs. Ryan looked over my shoulder. "Al's Delivery Service," she said. "Well, isn't that a coincidence? Look." She nodded at the kitchen window. Sure enough, Al was just pulling up outside Bub's house.

"Come on," said Yasmeen.

"Hey—" Mrs. Ryan followed us to the door. "Wouldn't you kids like a couple of toasted Christmas cookies?"

Chapter Nineteen

We turned down the cookies; we dashed out the door. We were so speedy that we arrived on Bub's porch only two steps behind Al. Luau was already there.

"'Afternoon, kids," Al said. "Coming for soup, too? Tuesday's minestrone. Means 'big soup' in Italian. Bub makes the biggest yet."

"We're detecting." Yasmeen sounded very serious. "We want to ask you some questions."

"Me?" Al said. And at that moment Bub's door opened.

"Hail, hail," said Bub, "right this way. Soup turned out real well. I've got coffee, too."

Al whispered to us. "Stay away from the coffee. It sits on the stove all day, just like the soup. For coffee, it's deadly."

I guess Yasmeen was so excited about detecting that she forgot about Bub's cooties and getting in trouble. She followed Al into Bub's house, no hesitation. I followed her.

The front door opened on a hallway. The picnic cooler Bub's niece had brought was sitting there. To the right was the living room, which also had a dining table. Beyond the table was the kitchen. Luau went right by the living room and up the hallway. Then he did the bump-bump-bump thing against a closed door on the left.

"Unh-unh, Mr. Kitty." Bub shook his head. "You stay outta there." He picked Luau up, carried him into the living room, and dropped him into the recliner by the TV. "Looks like Humphrey Bogart again," he said.

Al hung his coat on the back of a chair and sat down at the dining table. He cleared newspapers away to make space for himself.

Yasmeen and I hung back. Now that we were in, what were we supposed to do?

"Sit yourselves down, kids," Bub said from the kitchen.

"Did you know I'm a very important person?" Al said. "These kids have questions for me. *Detective* questions."

"Do tell." Bub came out with a bowl of soup, a spoon, and a paper towel. He set them on the table in front of Al. "Two more coming up."

Yasmeen and I argued, but Bub ignored us. Soon there were three bowls of soup on the table along with three paper-towel napkins. What else could we do? We sat down.

"The Queen of England won't be dining with us today," Bub said. "So there's no need to stand on ceremony. Eat up."

The soup smelled good. And I had missed lunch. "Good," I said between slurps. In fact, so good, I forgot about detecting.

But not Yasmeen. She ate one dainty bite and laid her spoon down. She pulled the cardboard ducky bottom out of her pocket. She held it up for Al to see. "Do you recognize *this*?" she asked him.

Yasmeen must have been watching movies like the one Luau was looking at now. I think she expected Al to break down and confess he was the bird thief, and maybe the Mouse thief, too. But he didn't. He took the cardboard from her and said, "Uh-huh. A piece cut out of one of my boxes. Where'd you get it?"

Yasmeen looked crushed. "You don't know?" she said.

Al pushed his bowl away. "Superb—as always," he told Bub.

"Got time for coffee?" Bub asked him.

Al was already standing and putting his coat back on. "Oh, no," he said. "Not this week. I got a delivery right here for Sophie and Byron—man, my sister buys them a lot of toys! Then I go downtown for Mrs. Miggins. After that, over the mountain to Belleburg for a pickup—all before three."

"Before you go," I said, "could I ask something?"

Al smiled. "Sure, if you make it snappy."

"Who besides you would have your boxes?"

"All kinds of people," he said. "The ones I just mentioned, for starters—the Sikora kids, Mrs. Miggins. . . . Probably everybody I deliver to has boxes kicking around. Why? Is that cardboard some kind of clue to something?"

"Some kind but not the good kind, I guess," Yasmeen said.

Al said he was sorry he couldn't help, and he headed for the door. Halfway across the room he nodded at the picture window. "Looky here who's coming up the walk," he said to Bub. "Guess the authorities have caught up with you at last."

Bub looked. "It was only a matter of time." He held his wrists out like he was ready for hand-cuffs. "I'll go quietly."

I heard footsteps on the porch, then Al opened the front door. "Hey, Officer," he said. "I gotta scoot, but the culprit says to come right in."

Chapter Twenty

Yasmeen and I looked at each other. What was going on? Was Bub really going to be arrested? Did this mean he was the thief, and Officer Krichels had solved the mystery already? That he had beaten Yasmeen and me?

Officer Krichels walked into the living room. He was tall and had a kind face, but now he looked stern. I expected him to pull out handcuffs, but instead he went over to the recliner and petted Luau. "This one's yours, right, Alex? Has he got a license?"

"Oh, now you need a license to watch a movie, do you?" Bub asked. "What's the world coming to?"

"I meant—" Officer Krichels started to say.

"I know what you meant," Bub said. "Want some soup?"

Officer Krichels smiled and took a seat next to me. "Why else would I be here?"

"You mean you're not going to arrest Bub?" Yasmeen said.

Officer Krichels laughed. "That coffee of his, it's a crime all right."

"Aw, what do cops know about coffee?" Bub said.

"Anyhow, your soup makes up for it," Officer Krichels went on. "Thanks very much."

Bub had set a bowl of soup in front of him. Officer Krichels wasted no time eating it. Meanwhile, I was trying to figure out what to do next. We would have to tell him about our evidence now. We didn't have any excuse not to. Yasmeen elbowed me, and I knew she was thinking the same thing.

"Uh . . . Officer Krichels?" I began. "We have something to tell you."

"I'm all ears," he said.

So I told him everything we knew—even the parts I hadn't told my mom yet. I told him about chasing the shape, finding the Mice with the milkmaids, the treasure map, the ducky's bottom. When I got to that last part, Yasmeen handed him the piece of cardboard. He took it but didn't study it the way I thought he should have. Finally, I was done talking, and he said, "Well, you kids have done some fine detective work, I must say. At the same time . . ." He scratched his head.

"What?" Yasmeen said.

"It's a little far-fetched, don't you think? Treasure maps? Mice hidden inside birds?"

"But we've got the evidence!" I said. "We can show you the map. It's at my house."

Officer Krichels nodded and smiled. "I'm sure you do, kids. The thing is, I've pretty much got it figured out on my own. Just as your mom thought, Alex, a kid prank."

"What!?" I said.

"How do you know?" Yasmeen said.

"Well, it *is* official police business," Officer Krichels said. "But I guess I can tell you. It should all be wrapped up neat this very afternoon. You see, the last lost bird has been found."

"Mr. Stone's calling bird?" Yasmeen said. "Where?"

Officer Krichels nodded. "In the birdbath."

"*What* birdbath?" Yasmeen asked.

But of course I already knew. There is only a single birdbath on our street. It's one of Luau's favorite hangouts. And it belongs to the Sikoras.

Chapter Twenty-one

Before Officer Krichels left, he explained how he knew about the lost bird. It was a tip, he said. And guess what? It came from my favorite blabbermouth friend, Russell. I bet he had been positively thrilled to phone the police about it.

Officer Krichels pulled his notebook from his pocket and studied what was written in it. "Our dispatcher, Angie Price, took this down," he said. "The informant, your friend Russell, called us shortly after noon today. It seems his brother, Graham, age five, was over at the Sikora residence this morning. It was Graham who observed the incriminating evidence, the calling bird, in the birdbath."

"That's weird," I said. "Graham and Byron Sikora are the same age. But usually they don't get along at all."

Officer Krichels shrugged. "I'm only telling you what was told to me," he said. "Anyhow, I'm now on my way to the Sikoras' to interview those kids. Sounds like one of them must be the perpetrator—the thief, I mean. I understand young Sophie has a bit of a reputation."

"But what about *our* evidence?" Yasmeen said. "The Mega-Menagerie burglary must be connected to the birds missing from the Twelve-Day display. Alex found those Mice in my yard. That's too big a coincidence."

Officer Krichels gave us one of those exasperating looks that grown-ups are always giving kids. "I've spent many a long year in the law enforcement game," he said. "And one thing I know is this: Coincidences happen."

"Can we come with you to interview Sophie and Byron?" Yasmeen asked.

Officer Krichels shook his head. "Official police business, kids. What if it got ugly? I can't put the law-abiding public—which in this case is you—at risk."

I was having a hard time imagining what kind of ugly Officer Krichels anticipated. Did he think Sophie and Byron might pull out their squirt guns? But he was already standing up to leave. There was nothing we could say.

When Officer Krichels was gone, Bub surprised me.

"Fred Krichels is a kind man and a good friend," he said. "But no one's ever accused him of being a brain. Personally, I thought you kids made a lot of sense."

"Thanks," I said.

Yasmeen looked sad, but then she smiled. "Anyway, Mr. Stone will be happy. And there's another good thing, too. We keep trying to share our evidence with the police. They keep not caring. So our detecting continues! Here's what I think, Alex. I think the time has come to write a list of suspects."

"You can do that only if you *have* a list of suspects," Bub said. "Do you?"

"Yeah—do we?" I echoed.

Yasmeen shrugged. "We will as soon as we make one."

Bub got up from the table and rooted around in a drawer. "I got a pencil and paper right here," he said. "I've seen my share of mysteries on TV. Maybe I can help." But before he found what he wanted, there were more footsteps outside, and the front door opened again.

"Wow," I said. "This place is as busy as a restaurant."

Bub smiled. "Credit our low, low prices."

The latest visitor turned out to be Jo, Bub's niece. As she fluttered around, removing her coat and mittens, she reminded me of a sparrow—small and quick.

I guess I had birds on the brain.

"Sorry I'm late," she said. "I had one last paper to turn in. It was about Polish Christmas traditions. Isn't that appropriate?"

"Hmmmph," Bub said.

"Bub's and my family came from Poland a long time ago," Jo explained. "Now that the paper's done, I can concentrate on the real thing: Christmas for Bub!"

Bub twirled one finger in the air. "Oh, joy."

Jo ignored him. "So, shall we get right to it?

I've got a lot to do before tomorrow. And besides, I don't want to lose my nerve." She nodded at the cooler.

Bub sighed. "If you say so," he said. "Kids, I'm sorry. I guess that list of suspects will have to wait. My niece and I have some business."

I felt embarrassed. Was there something he didn't want us to see? "Just let me get Luau," I said.

"Good idea," Bub said. "No telling what he'd do if he saw what Jo and I are up to."

We were barely out the door when Yasmeen made an announcement: "I have it all figured out."

"You do?" I said.

She nodded. "Mmm-hmm. I know what's in the bathtub. I know who stole the birds. I know *everything*."

"*Mrree-ow*," Luau said into my ear, and it meant "I know something, too, in case you were wondering."

So what else is new? I thought. Everybody's smarter than me, even my own cat. "Okay," I said. "Let's pretend I believe you. What?"

Chapter Twenty-two

Yasmeen might know everything, but she wasn't ready to tell me yet. First she wanted to make a detour to the Sikoras' backyard. I agreed. What kind of detectives would we be if we didn't take a look at that birdbath for ourselves?

Officer Krichels's car was still out front. I wondered what was going on inside the house. Had Sophie confessed? Was she really the thief? Is that what Yasmeen had figured out?

We stayed close to the Ryans' house as we jogged between it and the Sikoras' fence, where we could see into the backyard. We weren't precisely sneaking. But we didn't want anyone to look out and see us either.

Sure enough, when we looked over the fence, the calling bird was sitting in the birdbath. It looked very funny there. Funny and wrong. Why would the thief have put it there? All the other birds had been returned to their own flocks.

"Okay," I said when we were back on the sidewalk. "Explain."

Yasmeen grinned. It was a grin I didn't like much. "About how many Mice would fit into that picnic cooler?" she asked.

We walked up the sidewalk and into my front yard. We walked into my house, and I set Luau down. We took off our coats and hung them up. We found a note from my dad on the kitchen table: "Gone Christmas shopping. Back for dinner." We sat down.

All the time Yasmeen explained her theory to me. Bub had stolen the Mice from Mega-Menagerie and was keeping them in his bathtub. It was the Mice in the bathtub that Luau wanted. That was the reason he had been visiting Bub lately. The shape I chased last night? It was Jo. Hadn't I said the shape was small and quick? Anyway, that was why Bub seemed so eager to help us come up with our list just now. He wanted to make sure he wasn't on it.

The more Yasmeen talked, the sadder I felt. I didn't want it to be Bub. I kind of liked Bub. I definitely liked his soup.

But I remembered something. Two somethings. First, Bub had said he hated Christmas; second, he had said he liked jokes.

A joke was like a prank, right? Mom and Officer Krichels called the missing birds a "kid prank." Well, maybe they were half right. Maybe it was a grown-up prank. Maybe it had nothing to do with Mice. Maybe he was just mad at all the neighbors who called his house an eyesore, and this was a way to get back. I didn't think it was funny, but someone else might.

"Well," Yasmeen concluded. "What do you think?"

"I don't want it to be Bub," I said.

"Alex, we don't get to *pick* who it is," Yasmeen said. "It just *is* who it is. We can't let feelings get in the way. We have to look at the evidence. That's a detective's job."

"I never liked detecting," I reminded her.

"Anyway, let's do what you said before. Let's write a list. It doesn't have to be Bub. Officer Krichels thinks it's Sophie Sikora."

I got a pad and pencil out of the kitchen junk drawer. At the top I wrote "Suspects." Then, even though I didn't want to, I wrote "Bub and Jo." Then I wrote "Why?" And after that I wrote:

✳ Hates Christmas
✳ Likes pranks
✳ Mysterious cooler
✳ Luau likes bathtub

"Wait a minute," I said. "Luau started visiting Bub's last week, right? And bumping at the bathroom door?"

"He wanted the Mice," said Yasmeen.

I shook my head. "No, he didn't. Why would Luau care about a tub full of Super Macho Military Mice?"

"Because they're Mice!" Yasmeen said. "You know—cats, mice."

"Yasmeen," I said patiently. "They are not real Mice. No blood. No guts. None of that yummy stuff."

Yasmeen opened her mouth to argue. Then she closed it. My brilliant logic had stopped her. "Okay," she said after a minute. "If you're so smart, who did it?"

"Mr. Stone," I said, and I wrote that down.

"What?"

"You heard him at the Jensens' party. The Ryans' ducky has been driving him crazy for years. This year he just . . ." I snapped my fingers. "He probably stole the birds because he wanted everybody to get new ones, make their displays better."

"But who's the shape?" Yasmeen said. "Where's the connection to Mice?"

"His grandchildren," I said. "They don't live far away. One of them is probably the shape. Mr. Stone made the treasure map. He was hiding the Mice for them."

Yasmeen was thinking this over. I could see the wheels turn. Then she cocked her head. "Alex, get real," she said. "Can you seriously see an old, rickety man like Mr. Stone robbing a toy store? What did he do, climb in a window? No way."

I had to admit that was a problem. Still, I wrote down Mr. Stone on the list. And after "Why?" I wrote:

* Hates Ryans' ducky
* Give Mice to grandchildren
* Improve Twelve-Day birds

"Anyway," Yasmeen said while I wrote, "Mr. Stone gave us hot chocolate. He wouldn't give the detectives hot chocolate if he were the bad guy."

"By that logic, Bub's innocent, too," I said. "He gave us soup, didn't he? Besides, now you're letting *your* feelings get in the way."

"Am not," said Yasmeen.

I came dangerously close to saying, Are, too, which would have been just so pathetic.

But luckily I was stopped by the sound of the speakers outside: *"On the first day of Christmas, my true love gave to meee, a par-tridge in a pear treeee. . . ."*

Yasmeen grinned. Neither of us was tired of that music yet, even though the grown-ups were. To us kids, it always means Christmas.

"I have a different idea," Yasmeen said. "Let's phone Russell. I've been thinking about the calling bird in the bath—it doesn't fit. Where did it come from? Why did it show up this morning?

How come the thief didn't put it back with its own flock like he did with the other birds?"

"... *four calling birds* ..." sang the music helpfully.

I nodded. "Plus it doesn't make sense that Graham was over there. He thinks Byron's a crybaby. They never play together."

We went into the den so I could look up the number. From the den we could see the tourists outside. Among them tonight were Mrs. Miggins and Leo G. Luau had noticed them, too. He stood on the back of our sofa, swishing his tail.

I dialed the phone and asked to speak with Russell. When he came on, I told him we had talked to Officer Krichels. Then I asked him, "Since when does Graham hang out with Byron?"

"Since never," Russell said. "That lady at the police station? The one who wrote down what I said? I thought she sounded kind of confused. It was Billy Jensen who was over there. He saw the bird in the birdbath. He told Graham, and Graham told me. *I* knew it was evidence, so *I* called the police. Smart, huh?"

"Very smart," I assured him.

"Besides, Sophie wrecked my party. I didn't exactly mind turning her in. Did they arrest her? Did they put her in handcuffs and haul her away?"

I told him I doubted it, but if so, he could read it in the newspaper.

"Billy Jensen," Yasmeen repeated when I told her what Russell had said. "That little gossip. Leave it to him. Anyway, it reminds me. Michael was doing his own detecting. Remember? That's what he said when we saw him yesterday."

I nodded. "I gave him our first piece of evidence," I said. "But it doesn't matter now. We've got way better evidence than any old Mouse price tag."

"Maybe Michael knows something," Yasmeen said. "Maybe we should pool our information."

"You mean *share*?" I said. "No way. We're going to solve this ourselves. I think I've got it all figured out."

Yasmeen looked skeptical. "Mr. Stone?"

I shook my head. "Tiny miscalculation there."

"Okay, genius," she said, "what's the latest?"

I nodded at the window. Mrs. Miggins and Leo G. were looking at the nine drummers who drum nightly in the Snyders' yard. "Mrs. Miggins" I wrote on my list, and I held it up for Yasmeen to see.

"Fine with me," she said. "Nobody likes Mrs. Miggins. She's a witch. But why would she rob her own store?"

I explained what my mom had said about insurance scams. "The burglary was fake," I said. "She took the Mice herself, or somebody she knows did. Then she hid them away for a while. That explains how she arranged a Mouse delivery in time for Russell's party. That explains how she cleaned everything up so fast. Mom said the door wasn't even damaged."

I turned back to my list. "Why?" I wrote under "Mrs. Miggins." Then:

* Insurance money
* "Clean" burglary
* Got Mice fast

Yasmeen thought about what I had said. "Then, who's the shape?" she asked. "And why would Mrs. Miggins steal the birds or make a map?"

"I don't know," I admitted. "Maybe Sophie? Maybe Officer Krichels is right about that. Maybe there's something between Sophie and Mrs. Miggins? Sophie is fast. Maybe she was the shape."

"Fast but klutzy," said Yasmeen. "I can't believe she could run around the neighborhood on ice like that. She'd fall on her face."

"Or maybe Mrs. Miggins had another partner," I said. "But who?"

"Matt was trying to—what did you call it? Corner the market?" Yasmeen said. "Maybe it was him. He wants Mice more than anybody."

It was good and dark by now. We had spent the whole day detecting. We had collected all this great evidence. We had done all this great thinking. My poor brain ached. But, as far as I could tell, we weren't any closer to knowing who did it.

"Can we take a break?" I said. "I know. Let's go look at the Twelve-Day display. I haven't even walked around to see it at night this year."

Yasmeen agreed, and a few minutes later we were outside with the other tourists. Luau came, too. I guess he was afraid we might try to sneak in some detecting without him.

My idea was that seeing the decorations would help me think up an even more brilliant theory. But as soon as I saw them, I forgot all about crime and criminals. Even though I live with them every year, even though I know how unmagical they look in the daytime, I love seeing the Twelve-Day decorations at night.

Looking at them now, all I could think about was Christmas—only two days away.

Chapter Twenty-three

There were quite a few tourists that night. I said hi to Luke, one of the guys at Russell's party, and to Mr. Goh, who owns the gas station. In front of the McNitts' house we caught up with Michael and Billy Jensen. There was no point talking to Billy. He was singing along with something on his Discman. It sounded pretty bad with "The Twelve Days of Christmas" playing at the same time.

"Did you guys hear?" Michael asked us. "The police solved the case before I could. There goes my reputation."

"Don't feel bad," Yasmeen said. "It must have been a tough one."

"I do feel bad, though," Michael said, "because I was so far off. I had been thinking maybe Bub, because, well . . . you know. But the Sikoras had the calling bird—Billy saw it. I guess that's that."

I was afraid Yasmeen might argue with him. She can never resist arguing. To keep her quiet, I said the first thing that popped into my head. "Mr. Stone will be really glad to get that bird back—since his family made them and everything."

Michael laughed. "My mom says if she hears that story one more time—"

Now Yasmeen interrupted. She had to defend her new best bud, Mr. Stone. "But they *are* nicer than the other birds. Homemade, not plastic. And today he told us that one was special. His daughter made it."

"I wondered about the eyes," Michael said. "Why do girls like pink so much? Why isn't blue the girl color?"

That was a good question. I had never thought about it. But Yasmeen said it was a tradition, same as Christmas colors being green and red. "My mom could probably look up where it comes from," she said. "She's great at that."

While we were talking, Luau went over to see about Leo G. Being king and all, Luau expects any other animal that visits the neighborhood to bow, or at least stand still for a polite sniff. Unfortunately, Leo G. didn't know this. He is friendly to all creatures, even muscle-y orange cats. So when he saw Luau coming, he got all delighted and wagged his tail and stomped his front paws.

"Hey, Luau, watch out!" I tried to warn him.

But it was too late. Leo G. shook his big old slobbery head, and Luau was slime-sprayed from nose to tail.

"*Mrreeo-owowow!*" he hollered, and it meant "I have never been so humiliated!"

Yasmeen and I couldn't help it. We laughed till our tummies hurt. So did Michael and the other tourists in front of the McNitts' display. Only Billy and Mrs. Miggins missed out—Billy because of his Discman and Mrs. Miggins because she has no sense of humor.

"Your *cat* was annoying Leo G.," she said to me.

I gulped to stop myself from laughing. "Sorry."

Chapter Twenty-four

Yasmeen had to go home for dinner. "But I'll be over tomorrow at seven forty-five sharp," she said. "We need to work on our list. Tomorrow we solve the mystery!"

I didn't tell her I had one more name to add to the list: Yasmeen Popp. I didn't want to add it, but she was the one who said a detective has to look at the evidence, right? That a detective can't let feelings get in the way?

Back in the den, I wrote "Yasmeen." And under "Why?" I wrote:

* Person you least suspect
* Fast
* Ditched me to return swan?

So now there were four official suspects: Yasmeen, Mrs. Miggins, Mr. Stone, and Bub. Plus Officer Krichels's pick, Sophie Sikora. I looked at the list and shook my head. None of them seemed precisely right. We needed more evidence, but I didn't even know where to look.

"Anybody home?" Dad called.

"In here," I answered, and at the same time my stomach growled. Detecting was hungry work, and all I had eaten since noon was a bowl of soup. After Dad put his packages away, he fixed spaghetti for dinner. I was telling him how Officer Krichels thought Sophie was the bird thief, when Mom came home. She said hi, then went upstairs and changed into sweatpants, sweatshirt, and the fuzzy slippers I had given her for her birthday.

Back in the kitchen, she looked at her watch and said, "Want to see something funny?"

We followed her into the den, and she turned on the TV. There she was, on the screen, talking to Stan, the local news guy. "Detective Parakeet," Stan said, "is it fair to characterize this rash of burglaries as a holiday crime wave?"

"I don't think a sensational label serves the

public good, do you, Stan?" Mom said. "Toy mice have been taken from four stores in a fifty-mile radius of College Springs. That seems to be the extent of the crime wave."

"Should homeowners take additional security measures?" Stan asked.

"It's wise to be prudent," Mom said. "But I see no cause for alarm."

The station cut to a commercial for cat food. Luau hadn't come home yet. I figured he was looking for a beauty salon that stayed open late. It was too bad he had to miss this commercial, though. Some of the cats were very good-looking.

"Four stores?" I said to Mom. "So it wasn't only Mega-Menagerie."

"It's a Mouse crime wave," Mom said. "And you know what? Police remain baffled."

"Poor Mom," I said.

"Poor me," she agreed. "Hey—but on the bright side, Fred Krichels tells me he knows who stole the Twelve-Days of Christmas."

"Did Sophie confess?" I asked.

"Not exactly," Mom said. "She told him she didn't know anything about a calling bird in their birdbath, and her parents backed her up.

Then she had one of her tantrums, and of course they blamed poor Fred. Honestly, that child is so spoiled."

"But spoiled doesn't necessarily make her a thief," I said.

Dad looked at me. "You sound like you don't agree with Officer Krichels's assessment."

I told my parents Yasmeen and I had some evidence Officer Krichels didn't care about.

"Like what?" Mom said.

I hated that moment. She was looking at me and waiting. Not mad. Not yet. But I had a feeling she was going to be. I took a breath, then told her everything I should have told her last night—how I kicked over the milk pail, found the Mice, hid them in my bathrobe.

As I talked, I shrank. I thought if I were already tiny, she wouldn't need to yell so loud.

But shrinking didn't help.

"Alex Parakeet!" Mom exploded. "I have spent the day gallivanting around the countryside, while all the time you were sitting here with the best evidence we've got yet. . . . Don't you see? This changes the whole case!"

"Officer Krichels didn't think it mattered," I said in my tiniest voice.

"I will speak with Officer Krichels later," she said. "Now, bring me those Mice."

When I got back downstairs, Mom was lacing her shoes and talking on the phone. "Meet me downtown as soon as you can." She nodded at a plastic bag on the counter. I put the Mice in; she zipped it up. "Okay, see ya then—bye." She hung up.

"All this trouble for *toys*," she said to me. Then she looked at Dad. "Don't wait up. It may be another late night. Oh—and no more escapades, Alex Parakeet. Stay in your bed."

I nodded. I was hoping she'd give me a kiss or at least a smile before she left. But she just grabbed her jacket and mittens and walked out the door. She was really in a hurry. She was still wearing her sweats. She didn't even stop to put on makeup.

Chapter Twenty-five

I went to bed before Mom got back. My brain wanted to know what she found out, but my eyelids refused to cooperate. They kept falling shut. Luau had finally come home, and now he was curled up on my feet. He had done an amazing job cleaning off the slobber. He didn't even smell like Leo G. anymore. My dreams were terrible. I felt like Alice falling down the rabbit hole. The faces of the suspects whirled around me. The head of the Cheshire cat grinned.

Only this Cheshire cat had pink eyes.

I sat up so fast, I felt dizzy.

For a second I thought I was still spiraling

down the hole. Then I realized Luau wasn't on my feet. Is that what woke me? Luau jumping off the bed?

But wait—what was that horrible noise?

Oh, my gosh! "The Twelve Days of Christmas" at full volume! And the Twelve-Day lights were blazing, too! That must have been what woke me—the ultimate holiday alarm clock. By now everyone on Chickadee Court must be awake! What was going on?

I looked out the window. With the lights the street seemed bright as day. Nothing in our yard. Nothing on the sidewalk. Nothing at the Lees'. I ran to the bathroom, stood on the toilet, pushed the curtains aside. Now I could see the Popps' yard.

And that's where he was. A kid holding a milk bucket. A kid so still, he almost looked like another Twelve-Day decoration.

But on which day of Christmas did my true love give to me . . . Michael Jensen?

Mom had told me to stay in bed, but she hadn't counted on this. No one on all of Chickadee Court could stay in bed now.

I sprinted down the stairs and opened the

front door. Then I remembered my toes and had a good idea. Snow boots. They were by the front door. It took only a second to slide my feet in. Then out I ran, and as I jumped our front steps, I saw Yasmeen bursting out of her front door, too.

"ON THE SIXTH DAY OF CHRISTMAS . . ." the carol sang. Why was it so loud? What had turned it on in the middle of the night? What time was it anyway?

Yasmeen and I both ran straight at Michael, but before we got near, he dropped the bucket. The clatter when it hit woke him from his daze. He looked at me, then at Yasmeen. His face was terrified. In a flash, he turned and ran—right down the middle of the street.

I followed, but it was hopeless. In five seconds I was losing ground and out of breath. Tall, speedy Yasmeen kept gaining, though. Now they were halfway down the block, racing hard toward Michael's house. Other people were coming outside. I could hear shouting.

And then something scary happened.

Michael's grandparents' huge van was still parked in front of their house. As Michael approached, the headlights switched on; the motor roared; the tires squealed; the van lurched forward. Michael was far enough ahead to veer off and go around it—but Yasmeen hadn't caught up to him. The van barreled ahead.

It was coming right at her!

Chapter Twenty-six

My legs were slow. But my brain was in over-drive.

My best friend was about to be flattened.

Michael Jensen was the shape—and the bird thief.

And his grandparents—were they the Mega-Menagerie burglars?

I was running—eyes tearing, legs pumping, ribs aching—then all of a sudden I wasn't. I was flat on the cold, hard sidewalk—*ow!* The jolt shook every bone and scrambled my brain. What had happened? Darn that snow boot! It had slipped on an ice puddle, and my feet shot out from under me.

Now my whole body hurt. And my lips tasted salty—like blood.

But none of that mattered. *I* didn't matter. *I* wasn't the one about to be flattened. I rolled on my side and pushed up on a bruised elbow.

". . . NINE DRUMMERS DRUMMING, EIGHT MAIDS A-MILKING, SEVEN . . ."

The van kept coming. Yasmeen swerved right to get out of its path—but, unbelievably, the van swerved, too. Behind me, I heard my parents' voices. By now all the neighbors were running onto Chickadee Court—waving and yelling, trying to prevent the crash.

One person had a head start on them all. A slow person. A clumsy person. A person as big as a bear.

The collision happened in a blink, but I saw it all. In the headlights' glare the big-bear silhouette hit the skinny-kid silhouette; the skinny one flew up and away; the bear stopped and stood in the headlights, defiant, like one man's body could stop tons of metal.

A loud squeal. A colossal *thud*. A burnt smell.

"*Bub!*" I shrieked, just as Dad lifted me from the pavement.

". . . ELEVEN LADIES DANCING, TEN PIPERS PIP-
ING . . ."

Dad pulled me close and wrapped his arms
around me. I wanted to bury my head in his
shoulder and stay there. But that wouldn't
change anything. I had to look. There were
people clustered all around. I couldn't see Bub.
Was he bloody? Knocked flat? Dead?

"Bub!"

"Bub!"

"BUB!"

In all the voices I could make out Mr. Stone's
deep, grouchy one and Mrs. Blanco's, which was
high-pitched and squeaky.

Mrs. Lee kept repeating, "Are you all right?
Are you all right?"

Still carrying me, Dad ran toward the van. The
headlights remained bright. Someone had gone
around to the driver's side. I heard pounding.

"Ambulance on the way," Mrs. Ryan hollered.

Sirens—more noise on top of the music:
". . . SIX GEESE A-LAYING, FIVE GOLDEN RINGS,
FOUR . . ."

Someone laughed—that was weird—Mr.
Stone. "Look it here—in the back," he said.

"Better get Detective Parakeet around to see this. And I suspect the kids'll be interested."

As we got closer, I heard something else, something wonderful: Bub's voice, weak but gruff as ever.

"No, Mrs. Lee . . . I am *not* . . . all right," he was saying. "It hurts . . . being hit . . . by a truck."

Behind us, Mom breathed a sigh. "Oh, thank heavens."

Finally, Dad pushed through. There was Bub on the street. The van must have hit him at an angle. He was off to its right side, half of him in the headlight's beam. He was leaning back on his elbows, shielding his eyes from the glare with his hand. He was wearing striped pajamas. The top was bloody. So were his hands. I couldn't see where the blood came from. His face was pale. He was barefoot. His toes were white and ugly.

It was mean to notice toes at a time like this. But I couldn't help it.

Professor Jensen stood closest to him. He was talking, but I couldn't hear words. Mrs. Jensen was nowhere around. Neither were Michael and Billy.

And where was Yasmeen? *How* was Yasmeen?

I looked over by where she had landed. Too many people. I couldn't see. How hard had she fallen?

Now there was commotion around the driver's door; it opened; my mom took over.

"Gangway, ladies and gentlemen," she said. "All right, step out of the vehicle, please. Hands where I can see them."

". . . AND A PAR-TRIDGE IN A PEAR TREE."

With that, the Twelve-Day lights went dark and the music silent. It was almost as big a shock as when they flashed on. For a moment the street was black except here in the headlights. Then the porch lights at the Ryans' popped on. And after that the lights at the Jensens' and the McNitts'. Mom reached into the van and shut down the headlights. My teary eyes were grateful.

The sirens came nearer. Dad put me down. I knelt next to Bub. "Do you hurt a whole lot?" I asked.

"Ah, yup." His voice was wheezy, like he couldn't get his breath. It was scary—this big, powerful guy suddenly seemed so fragile. "You're not . . . lookin' so good," he said, "either."

I wiped my hand across my lip. Blood. Yuck. "I tripped."

"Klutz," he said. "What happened . . . to your sidekick?"

I looked around for her again. This time I found her, walking toward us. She was limping, leaning on her dad. There were tear streaks on her face. But there was a brave smile, too. She was okay.

I don't think I've ever felt so relieved. I stood up, ready to give her a big hug. But of course I didn't. Too embarrassing.

Professor Popp nudged her toward Bub. "How do you feel?" she asked him.

"You don't . . . want to know," Bub said.

"My dad says you saved my life."

Bub took one wheezy breath, then two. He shrugged and grimaced. "Better me down here . . . than you."

Yasmeen's teary eyes brimmed over. "I'm really sorry," she said. "Are you going to—?"

Bub shook his head. "No, I'm not . . . going to," he said. "And don't you be . . . sorry. The darn driver . . . should be sorry."

Which reminded me, who was the darn

driver? I looked up at the van. There was Mom, helping whoever it was out.

Now I saw: It was Michael's grandma! I recognized her happy-face sweater.

What kind of grandma tries to run over kids in the street?

Mom slammed the van door, which made Michael's grandma jump. With Mom holding her arm, they walked toward the sidewalk. I couldn't see Grandma's face, but from the back she looked shaky, slow, and small. I didn't see Grandpa at all.

Now the sirens got even louder—the ambulance had turned the corner onto Chickadee Court. Right behind it were a fire truck and two police cars.

Every one of them wailed. We couldn't hear each other talk. The red lights made everything flash pink.

The ambulance pulled alongside the van. It had barely stopped when three guys sprang out, two carrying a stretcher. From radios blared a lot of official-sounding talk—code numbers, car numbers.

I put my hands over my ears. It didn't help. It was the loudest night of my life.

"Outta the way, please," hollered an ambulance guy. "Give the patient some air; all right now; what have we got?"

The other ambulance guys hooked Bub up to wires and tubes. It seemed like no time till they had slid him into the back; then the siren wailed again, and the ambulance rolled away toward the hospital.

I was worried about Bub, afraid for him. But soon I was distracted, too. There had never been so much action on Chickadee Court.

Chapter Twenty-seven

Yasmeen and I found a place to sit on the sidewalk and watch. Police swarmed everywhere. Firefighters herded people farther away from the van. A patrol officer put yellow police tape around it. More officers were asking the neighbors questions.

This was kind of funny, I thought. Here were Yasmeen and I, the only ones who knew what had happened and why. Nobody was asking us anything.

"We should have figured it out sooner," Yasmeen said. "Remember by the McNitts' tonight, when Michael said—"

"Pink eyes." I nodded. "I know."

"Shoot," Yasmeen said. "I *hate* it when you're as smart as me."

"Get used to it," I said. "But I only figured it out just now. You can't see the calling bird's eyes unless you're close to it. That's what Mr. Stone told us. And the only person who got close to the bird was the bird thief."

"Ergo," Yasmeen said, "Michael was the bird thief. Remember how he's been yawning so much?"

"Oh—and he was subbing on that *paper* route! I bet it was easy to swipe birds while he was delivering newspapers in the dark."

"Right," said Yasmeen. "But there's still one thing I'm confused about—the milk bucket. Why did he go back for it tonight?"

For once I knew something she didn't. "Because he thought the Mice were still in it," I said, "the ones from last night. That's where he hid them when I was chasing him."

"And then you stole them," Yasmeen couldn't help reminding me.

"And *then* I gave them to my mom as evidence," I said.

Yasmeen smiled. "Good for you," she said. "But I bet she was mad."

"Oh, boy, was she. Anyway, so Michael followed the treasure map. And the treasure map was made by—"

"Grandma!" We said it at the same time.

"But what about Grandpa?" said Yasmeen.

"Don't know," I admitted. "But I bet he was involved, too. Even as tough as Grandma is, I can't see her robbing Mega-Menagerie—"

"—and those other stores, too, don't forget—"

"Right. I can't see her doing that by herself."

"So Grandma must have hidden a few of the stolen Mice in the birds for Michael to find," Yasmeen said.

"Weird."

Yasmeen shrugged. "Maybe not. Even criminals love their grandkids. She was trying to give him some fun, a Christmas present."

"Yeah," I said. "And also his parents wouldn't let him have Mice. So she couldn't just wrap 'em and put 'em under the tree. She had to be sneaky."

Yasmeen nodded. "But isn't Michael kind of old to play with Mice?"

"How can you say that?" I said. "Mice are for all ages! And anyway, you know how grandparents are. They think kids are babies practically forever. But I've got another question. We know it was Michael who put the calling bird in the Sikoras' birdbath. But why? I don't get it."

"What about this?" Yasmeen said. "What if you scared him last night? And he thought he had to do something fast to throw you off the track? So what he did was put the calling bird at the Sikoras' house. He knew Billy would see it when he went over today."

I nodded. "I get it. Knowing Billy, Michael could be sure the information would get spread around. And everybody knows about Sophie. . . ."

"I feel sort of bad about Sophie now," Yasmeen said. "Nobody should assume another person's a thief just because they're different— well, troublesome. That's what we all did with Bub, too."

I wasn't worried about Sophie. I was too busy feeling bad about something else. I shouldn't have put Yasmeen on the list of suspects. If I couldn't trust my best friend who happened to be a girl, who could I trust? Detecting was not only hard work, it was dangerous, too. It made you too suspicious. If I ever did any more detecting, I would have to watch out for that.

"So now there's only one mystery left," said Yasmeen.

"There is?"

"Hellooo?" Yasmeen knocked on my skull. "Don't you remember? We still don't know what was in Bub's bathtub!"

By now the street had quieted down. So when a police car's engine turned over, we jumped. Through the back window I could just see Michael's grandma, looking very small. Officer Krichels was driving. Mom thumped the roof with her fist as it pulled away. "Meet you downtown," she said.

I smiled and shook my head. Sometimes Mom is so incredibly cool.

There was more laughter from behind the van; I remembered how I heard Mr. Stone laugh before. What was that about?

"Let's look," I said to Yasmeen.

I had to help her up. We walked around the van, with her leaning on me. People smiled at us, and I felt important, like someone who has been supporting an injured hero for years and years now.

A knot of people—Mrs. Dagostino, Mr. Ryan, Mr. and Mrs. Swanson—were clustered around the back of the van. We pushed through till we ran into the police tape.

In the crash, the van's doors must have popped. They hung open still. And now that we could see what had flown out—we started laughing, too.

Chapter Twenty-eight

Chickadee Court looked like a battlefield, with dead and wounded lying everywhere, most still clinging to their weapons. It might not sound funny. But it was. Because these soldiers had big pink ears.

Seeing a billion Super Macho Military Mice all at once, I couldn't help it. I felt a surge of greed. Why not scoop up a few?

But my greed didn't last.

I knew I couldn't actually steal them. I had found out that guilt made stealing not worth it. I wondered about Michael's grandma. She had stolen all those Mice. And she was old. Hadn't she ever learned about guilt? Or maybe she didn't feel any. If you don't, does that mean you don't have a conscience? If nobody had a conscience, what would the world be like?

Well, one thing, nobody would put up Christmas displays. The birds and lights and speakers wouldn't be safe. Stuff would go missing every time it got dark.

I was thinking these deep thoughts, Yasmeen leaning on my arm, when I saw Mrs. Jensen walk toward us. For once she didn't look perfect. No lipstick and her face was streaked, tears maybe. Like Grandma, she looked sort of shrunken. But that wasn't embarrassment. It was the size of what she was carrying: a big, muscle-y orange cat, Luau.

"What is with the ace detective now?" Yasmeen asked.

"He's yours, I think?" Mrs. Jensen handed him to me.

I put him over my shoulder and nodded.

"*Mrrr-ow*," Luau said. And it meant "Don't drop me. I've been through enough for one day."

"Where did he come from?" I asked.

Mrs. Jensen shrugged. "I'm not positive, but I *think* he's responsible for the late-night lights and music."

"Luau?!" I said. "How . . . ?"

Mrs. Jensen looked at Yasmeen. "Oh, honey," she said. "I am *so sorry.* . . ." She sniffed and wiped her nose. I was scared she was going to cry. It is awful when grown-ups cry.

Yasmeen must have been scared, too. "I'm okay," she said quickly. "I mean, I'll be okay. It isn't your fault . . . uh, exactly."

Mrs. Jensen tried to smile. "There'll be time for explanations, for apologies," she said. "But for now . . . this cat. I found him curled up on the bookcase in the living room—the one by the switch? All I can think is he came in when Michael went out. Then he jumped up and his tail brushed it—something like that. It's rather funny, isn't it? I mean—oh, dear—if any of this is funny. The cat woke up the whole neighborhood. Then he fell fast asleep."

Chapter Twenty-nine

You might think I could have slept in the next morning. I mean, it was almost dawn when I collapsed into bed. It was Christmas Eve. All our detecting was done.

So what was there possibly to wake me up early?

The phone.

It rang and rang. Don't you think parents should answer when kids are in bed? Shouldn't that be a law, like the Bill of Rights and stop signs?

Anyway, my parents didn't. And the ringing didn't end till the machine picked up. I rolled over. The ringing started again. Maybe it was the hospital. Something to do with Bub?

"Hello?" I yawned into the receiver. "Is Bub okay?"

But it wasn't the hospital at all. It was Stan, the news guy from TV. He had called Yasmeen already, but she said she wouldn't talk to him unless I was there, too. She said we solved the case together, and it was only her dumb luck that she was the one that got almost run over and became a hero.

You never saw anybody as happy as Stan when he came to interview us later. It was a once-in-a-lifetime Christmas story, he said. Heartwarming! Funny! With just that holiday dash of pathos!

I didn't know what pathos was either. Yasmeen told me "sadness." So why didn't he just say sadness?

Anyway—the stories will be all over the paper tomorrow, and they've been on TV and radio and the Web today:

"Elderly Hero Risks Life, Saves Child"

"Reckless Driver Arrested as Mouse Thief"

"Who Stole the Twelve Days of Christmas? Ask Grandma!"

By the end of the day practically everybody on Chickadee Court had been interviewed. Everybody except Bub, that is, because his doctors kept the reporters away. And the Jensens. They wouldn't talk to anybody. Who could blame them? I wondered how Michael was doing. I guessed now he wouldn't be king of the neighborhood anymore.

Anyway, he wouldn't have to go to jail, Mom said. It wasn't his fault he had criminal grandparents.

"So his grandfather was in on it, too?" I asked her.

"He was the one who knew about locks and keys," Mom said. "They used to have a lock shop. Apparently Jon—Professor Jensen—set them up in this new business, Tabby Antiques and Junque. They've never had much money. I don't know, maybe they were jealous of Jon's success. Anyway, when they saw how valuable the retired Mice were, they decided to grab as many as they could and put them away till prices rose. By then the burglary cases would be cold—"

"Cold?" I interrupted.

"So old, they're hard to solve," Mom explained. "And then they'd feel safe putting the Mice out at their store."

"Well, I think we were all perfectly stupid not to figure it out sooner," said Dad. "The van was sitting on our street for days. Anyone who spells 'junk' with a 'q' is obviously some kind of a criminal."

Mom pulled me close and messed up my hair. It sort of drives me crazy when she does that. I am not some little kid anymore. Still, it was better than laser death stares. "I know it was hard to confess to me about the Mice," she said. "I know how much you like them. And we can't give you stuff like we used to when your dad was working."

"It's okay, Mom," I said. "I don't think I like them so much now anyway. Seeing a whole pile of them in the street? It's sort of like seeing the Twelve-Day display in the daytime. They don't seem magical anymore."

"Uh-oh," Dad said. "Not even Ulysses S. Mouse?"

From the way he said it, I had a pretty good

idea what I was getting for Christmas. "Well, sure I still want *that* one," I said.

"Thank goodness," said Dad.

Mom gave me a squeeze. "You're not bad for a kid, Alex."

From Mom, this was a pretty good compliment. I asked another question. "What about Leo G.? How did they get by him?"

"That pussycat?" Mom said. "He's not much of a watchdog. Grandma just brought him a dog biscuit is all."

"No wonder he was so glad to see her when she dropped Billy at the Mouse party," Dad said.

"So what about last night?" I asked. "What was Grandma trying to do anyway?"

"Make a getaway." Mom laughed, then covered her mouth. "I'm sorry. I know Bub was injured, and that's a shame. But there is a comical side. When the lights went on and caught Michael in the act, she panicked. She ran straight for the van with the Mice in it. She didn't stop for Grandpa. Or her glasses."

"So she couldn't see?" I asked.

"She wasn't trying to hit anybody; at least

that's her story. She never saw Yasmeen at all, only Bub. And she braked as soon as she saw him."

You will never believe what we did that night—Christmas Eve. We celebrated at Bub's house with a traditional Polish Wigilia, which is pronounced *Vi-jeel-ya* because it's Polish, and the Poles are almost as bad spellers as the French.

My dad thought Bub was crazy when he called from the hospital to invite us.

"Excuse me," Dad said, "but aren't you the guy who was mowed down by a five-ton motor vehicle in the middle of the night?"

"Ah, yup," Bub said. "But they're springing me . . . at three o'clock. So long as you're in one piece . . . they don't let you . . . lie around."

"Bub, forgive my saying so, but you don't sound so good."

"Clean bill . . . of health," Bub said. "Anyway . . . my niece Jo . . . is doing the work. I'll just sit on the divan . . . in the splendor . . . befitting a hero."

Jo invited Yasmeen's family for Wigilia, too. Yasmeen got permission, but her parents said no thanks. They said Jeremiah couldn't be trusted to behave at a dinner party. But really I think they were embarrassed to come. All these years they bad-mouthed Bub. Now he had gone and saved Yasmeen's life.

Luau came along, too, of course. When Jo welcomed us, he walked in, tail flying. And he leapt to his usual spot on the recliner as if it were his personal throne.

"Meow!" he said when he was settled. And it meant "Let's see what's tasty on TV!"

Jo was wearing a short green dress and fancy shoes. She was grinning. She looked pretty. Bub was on the sofa. His face was papery white; there were bandages on his hands; he was smiling, too.

"Ho . . . ho . . . ho," he said.

"Take a look at that table!" said my dad.

"Take a look at that fish!" said my mom.

There was a white cloth on the table; there was a feast of food laid out, most of it weird stuff I never saw before. Weirdest of all was a whole fish! With the head and the eyes and everything! It was dead. My stomach did a flip-flop. Were we supposed to eat *that?*

At the same moment I saw the fish, the wind must have shifted. Luau sniffed the air; he hopped down from the recliner; he strolled toward the table.

"*Meow?*" he said innocently. Then he jumped onto a chair and leaned back on his haunches, ready to spring.

"Oh, no, you don't." Jo grabbed him. "We'll save you the tail and the eyeballs, too—if you're good."

"Eyeballs are . . . the best part," said Bub. "Anyway . . . Luau's . . . been darn patient. He deserves . . . the treat."

"Wait a minute." Yasmeen looked at me. "Is it the *fish* that was in the bathtub?"

Bub nodded. "Only it was . . . livelier then."

"But why keep a fish in the bathtub?" Yasmeen asked.

Jo explained as we sat down at the table. The fish was a carp, traditional for Christmas Eve in Poland. It wasn't a kind of fish you could buy at American grocery stores. She had gone to a lot of trouble to find one.

"Isn't a carp a goldfish?" Dad asked.

We were going to eat a goldfish?

Jo laughed. "Only a goldfish cousin," she said, which didn't make me feel that much better.

"Most Polish people are Catholic," she explained. "On Christmas Eve they don't eat meat. So they eat carp. It's hard to get fresh fish right before Christmas. So people buy them live and keep them in the bathtub. It's part of the tradition."

"We didn't want you . . . to see us . . . killing the fish," Bub said, "not . . . at your tender age."

Now I understood. "That's why you asked us to leave the other day!"

Yasmeen winced. "You killed him? And put his poor dead carcass in the cooler?"

Jo made a face. "It wasn't pretty."

"I'm sure he had a happy life," said Dad. "And now he looks delicious. Shall we eat?"

"Not yet!" said Jo. She told us first there was a ritual called sharing the *oplatek*, which is pronounced *oh-pwa-tek*. Oplatek are very thin crackers with Christmas pictures stamped on them. What you do is wish each person something special, then trade pieces of cracker.

I thought it sounded stupid.

But it turned out to be nice.

Mom wished me to stay a great kid.

Dad wished me to stay helpful around the house.

Jo wished me to be a good friend to her uncle.

And Bub wished me a long and happy childhood.

Then it was Yasmeen's turn. "I wish us both another mystery to solve!" she said.

"You're kidding," I said. Wasn't that the last thing I wanted? Didn't I hate detecting?

Except maybe I didn't. It had been fun to have something to think about besides Lousy Luigi. Fun to do something real.

And maybe the next mystery would happen in the spring or the summer, sometime when the weather was warm.

It was my turn to wish something for Yasmeen. I could see she was impatient—eager to eat goldfish, I guess.

"I wish you the same thing," I said. "Another mystery!"

We high-fived. And Luau meowed. This time it meant "Merry Christmas!"